"Shh!" As she raised a fingertip to her lips, he caught her hand and kissed that finger.

"Gabby...if you have coffee with me, there's a chance I'll kiss you again."

Wiggling her hand free of his grasp, she said, "Kiss me again and people are going to start talking."

"Then let's go someplace where they're not watching." Geoffrey was all good with letting her lead him out of the Pearl and to an elevator that brought them to the third floor. Their destination was a balcony lined with plants. Just before the balcony was an intimate room that housed vending machines—one being a self-serve espresso machine.

"You said coffee," she reminded him, plucking two foam cups. "This is where staff members occasionally go for self-sentenced time-outs."

Vending-machine espresso in hand, they went to the balcony.

"We can say nothing at all, or figure out what we're doing here," she finally said. "Either way, we can't be making this into some routine."

"Since I walked out of the restaurant yesterday, it's been nothing but you. In my head, all night, and I can't change it. I'm chained here."

Dear Reader,

I never considered myself a creative person until someone told me I was. Knowing this, then you surely can understand why I don't think I have a creative process. For me, writing is more of an *intuitive* process. I follow my gut instead of specific steps to create a result. I thrive on inspiration—and most enjoy it when it comes unexpectedly. But I'd quite like to marry intuition and creativity, and discover what I come up with.

Perhaps I can take notes from Gabrielle Royce, the heroine in *Hot Summer Nights*. Intuition and creativity (and a love for rock music!) make Gabby one of the most dazzlingly eccentric and skilled chefs in the biz. She's in touch with every facet of her personality—until Geoffrey Girard gives her a taste of lust and tempts her to come back for *much* more.

Read. Eat. And rock on.

XOXO

Lisa Marie Perry

HOT
SUMMER
NIGHTS

LISA MARIE PERRY

HARLEQUIN® KIMANI™ ROMANCE

Recycling programs
for this product may
not exist in your area.

ISBN-13: 978-0-373-86409-6

Hot Summer Nights

Copyright © 2015 by Lisa Marie Perry

HARLEQUIN®

Printed in U.S.A.

™ www.Harlequin.com

Lisa Marie Perry thinks an imagination's a terrible thing to ignore. So is a good cappuccino. After years of college, customer service gigs and a career in caregiving, she at last gave in to buying an espresso machine and writing to her imagination's desire. Lisa Marie lives in America's heartland, and she has every intention of making the Colorado mountains her new stomping grounds. She drives a truck, enjoys indie rock, collects Medieval literature, watches too many comedies, has a not-so-secret love for lace and adores rugged men with a little bit of nerd.

Books by Lisa Marie Perry

Harlequin Kimani Romance

Night Games
Midnight Play
Just for Christmas Night
Mine Tonight
Hot Summer Nights

Visit the Author Profile page at
Harlequin.com for more titles.

For Susie—

We've been through a lot and have the scars to prove it.
Thanks for a wild ride.

Chapter 1

"When was the last time you faked it?"

Visions of uncomfortably thorough interviews that left her feeling naked, judged and stripped of her ego, and a few unfortunately memorable occasions of substandard sex came easily to Gabrielle Royce's mind. *Too* easily. "Faked it?" She darted smoothly through the restaurant's busy stadium-size kitchen to join the classically trained sous-chef and celebrity pastry chef in front of a stainless steel counter. "Confidence? Orgasms? What are we talking about faking here?"

"Dessert." The sous-chef indicated the lone plate on the counter, clearly speaking up for *Hollywood's Hardcore Baking Challenge* alum Nicola Joon, the pastry chef who could be belligerently bold on her top-rated reality baking show, *Confection Affection X*, but in *actual* reality stood subdued to silence, humbled by a trio of what might be champagne-glazed crème brûlée poppers. "When was the last time you faked culinary genius because you didn't want to accept that what you created was no more special than a store-bought snack?"

"Never. A girl can fake her way through a lot of things, and with damn good reason, but when it comes to food there's no point. Food always speaks for itself, and it's louder than any chef's nonsense." Gabrielle was a chef beyond occupation. She experienced and understood food, and demanded more from it than sustenance. For her, cooking was all or nothing. It had to be. At twenty-eight, she had no unforgivable regrets—after a good month of tattoo remorse, she'd even come to cherish the blowing dandelion inked on her left shoulder blade—yet she'd sacrificed more than most people realized just for the chance to study the nuances of culinary arts and put her stamp on the leisure and hospitality industry.

"You've got one of the most critical palates in the biz, Gabby." Nicola handed her a polished fork. The round shape and bite size suggested it was an eat-with-your-fingers dessert, an interesting coupling of gourmet elegance and down-to-earth comfort, but after two weeks of studying Gabrielle's technique, flair and quirks she must've detected that as a practice Gabrielle didn't taste without utensils. "Be brutal."

"How brutal?"

"Bitch brutal. Do your worst."

Gabrielle took the fork, twirled it between her fingers. "Nicola, do you truly think it's no more unique than 'store-bought'?"

"Truly, I haven't formed an opinion. I thought I'd reserve that honor for you."

"And you, Shoshanna?" She addressed the sous-chef hanging on her every syllable. A seasoned professional deserving of her own glory, Shoshanna Smirnov avidly believed that only by mastering a craft did one reach a point where they could start to actually learn it. A student of the kitchen, now and forever. Gabrielle had to admit she liked that about her. "Have you sampled one?"

"No, Nicola cake-blocked me."

Allowing a soft snort, Gabrielle said, "It's not cake, is it? It's crème brûlée that took a bath in champagne. Am I close, Nicola?"

Nicola nodded. "You didn't send spies to my workstation, did you?"

"No. All hands are on deck today, so nobody's spying." Their most versatile line cook on staff had called in sick, which was why Gabrielle had delegated herself to the kitchen for the entire morning and much of the afternoon. Come hell or high water, the restaurant couldn't skip a beat. "But now I'm intrigued. Am I looking at an authentic Nicola Joon pâtisserie prototype?"

"This could be the Pearl's new signature dessert, if you think it's acceptable to introduce to the pastry team."

"At the Belleza, it's not *acceptable* if it's not *perfection*," Gabrielle reminded her. It was the mind-set that had earned her the executive chef position at California's most exclusive resort and had catapulted her career to a peak that afforded her the clout to cherry-pick guest chefs and burdened her with the kind of attention that had celebrities interested in seducing her into their kitchens. But if there was anything as iron-strong as Gabrielle's backbone, it was her loyalty to the Belleza—and the Parkers, a family of brilliant minds who were relying on her visions of edge and class to lead the resort's award-winning restaurant, the Pearl, into a new era.

"When would you say a dessert has reached perfection?" Shoshanna asked.

Gabrielle rolled a popper onto her fork, considered the artistic beauty of the fragile dessert before arching a brow at the sous-chef, who pinched one off the plate. "When it triggers an emotional response. Or an orgasmic experience. On three?"

"Three."

She closed her eyes, counted, then let its tantalizing aroma and airy texture contribute to her impression of the dessert's taste. A drop of citrus in the center was an unexpected burst of flavor that sent a delicate shiver directly down her spine. Heaven *had* to taste like this.

She laid down her fork. "I want this to cuddle with me tonight and call me tomorrow."

"*Bozhe moi!* This is all the satisfaction I need," Shoshanna said. "If I wasn't worried about calories jumping like paratroopers to my hips, I'd consider eating this every day and giving up my bob."

"Bob?" the others asked.

"You American girls, act like you know," she teased. "Bob. *Bob.* Battery-operated boyfriend."

Their evaluation of the sinfully satisfying pastry was interrupted with "Don't walk backward. Dangerously hot garlic saffron broth coming through." The words, accompanied with the harsh footsteps of the harried chef carting a large stockpot haloed with billowing steam, brought back the realities of the hectic kitchen. Gabrielle searched for innovative ways to reduce stress and promote a positive environment, but even the Pearl's staff fell prey to the pressures of providing five-star excellence to the world's elite.

Grateful that Nicola's dessert had allowed her to escape the stress for a few minutes, she nodded her approval to the chef. "Great start, but it needs refining. Perhaps we can experiment with the citrus? Before we get the pastry team fired up, let's play with the recipe. Our produce supplier has a soft spot for this kitchen. We can drive out and consider more options. We'll make a field trip of it."

"Would that soft spot be for the Pearl, or for you?" Chef Stu Merritt jibed as he passed them. Gabrielle had met Stu in London and had considered it a personal win that the Belleza had tempted him to add his seafood expertise to the Pearl. A seven-foot hulk, he cloaked Gabrielle with his shadow as he paused at the workstation. She could pass as average height only in her most ambitious high heels. "There has to be a reason we're getting the best produce in California and the delivery blokes splash on cologne before they get you to sign their forms."

"The Belleza requires we work with the best ingredients. Our current suppliers happen to provide that and a pleasant *business* relationship. As far as personal relationships go, cologne and high-quality organic produce are nice, but what gal wouldn't ask for more? I'm harder to get than that." This was met with a clipped nod and an unconvinced grunt, but no further debate from the chef. Still, Gabrielle picked up on the curi-

ous glance between Nicola and Shoshanna as if it were
the strike of a shaft of light against a gem. "Okay, I'm
sensing either of you has something to add. Is there
something you want to add?"

"You mean to say there's no...ah—" Shoshanna
wrung her pale hands, causing the scatter of faint blue
veins to appear more vibrant under her skin "—overlap
between your business and personal relationships?"

"As in business with benefits? No. To maintain the
integrity of this kitchen and the Pearl, I don't allow *that*
kind of overlap. If you're affiliated with the Belleza,
you'd better believe that where you're concerned there's
an invisible bear trap between these legs." An A plus
policy, she figured. In a delicate position as a twenty-
eight-year-old executive chef at a resort owned by the
family of one of her closest friends, she had enough
potential vulnerabilities to draw tabloid attention without courting sex scandals. She didn't need anyone—the
press, the staff she managed, her friends and especially her family—to open their ears to gossip. So to
minimize the probability of stirring up media hell and
then paddling her way to redemption, she was "Sorry,
I'm closed" when it came to getting intimate with colleagues, members of the press and Belleza guests.

"But Kimberly Parker is engaged to Jaxon Dunham.
The Dunhams are some of the resort's most high-profile
clients," Shoshanna persisted. "The precedent's already
there. Besides, since your life is all about the Belleza,
the only way to save yourself from seeing that invisible bear trap turn into cobwebs is to add a little play
to your work."

Gabrielle started to scoff, but Shoshanna was picking up momentum. "*Daversya mne*, I know volumes

about romance. Ask any of my lovers. The Belleza does not need your entire life. We want to share you." She snapped her fingers, beamed a photo-perfect smile. "I know—you'll hook up with the next sexy eligible man you see."

"Don't look at me," Stu said, backing away with his tattooed arms up as if to hold her off, his eyes wide through his fuchsia-framed glasses. "I've taken you out for ale before, Chef Royce. You could drink a pub bankrupt. And pie isn't my preferred dessert."

"Funny, Chef Merritt. So funny."

"Dry sarcasm. Always dry sarcasm. Why don't you laugh more often? I don't know any male who wouldn't fall half in love with your laugh."

"I'm too busy to laugh," she said, freeing her curly hair from its nets, untying her apron and gearing up to check on the Pearl's dining room. All morning she'd fluttered from one kitchen task to another, filling in wherever she was needed while still juggling her executive chef duties. "And I don't want a male who's only half in love with me."

If I wanted to settle for "halfway" and "sort of," I would've stayed in my family's world and lived a life that'd make me half *happy.*

The coarse, comfortable banter of this kitchen was something she appreciated. As for the aha moment that made it clear that every member of her crew knew she had no man—not so much. "I'm choosing to blame Kimberly for the direction of this conversation, but let me end it with this. Unlike her, I would never get involved with a guest. Things can get messy fast. The Belleza's been through too much recent drama already. I won't invite more."

The Pearl, in particular, had faced the brunt of that drama. A rash of guests complaining about food poisoning…numerous harsh reviews on several popular travel websites…speculation that had wrinkled the Belleza's stellar reputation and had forced Gabrielle to suspect that any day her employers might tear her a new one or cut her from the resort's staff.

She'd hated wearing that uneasiness, could hardly stomach wondering when the women who'd been her friends since their Massachusetts private school days, Kimberly Parker and Robyn Henderson, might turn on her for the good of the resort. The Parkers owned the Belleza and their histories were intertwined, yet each of the three friends now carried high-level positions and had a stake in its prosperity. Over a span of several decades the resort had endured everything from a grim 1980s recession to whispers of buried treasure, from ownership carousels to rumors of what she'd heard Shoshanna call bad omens.

In a shocking business maneuver that had turned siblings into adversaries, Kimberly's parents had named her general manager—not her brother, the Parker heir who'd been groomed to be the successor. Robyn was the Belleza's lead event planner, who took every success personally and flat-out believed failure wasn't an option. And as executive chef of the Pearl, Gabrielle was caught between two violently ambitious people— Kim, a friend who'd had her back since way back when, and Kim's brother, a guy she admired and whose job Gabrielle had swiped three years ago.

But, somehow, a seed of suspicion that the woman responsible for keeping the upper crust clientele wined and dined was in fact incompetent despite immaculate credentials had caused the foundation of what kept this place running—trust—to buckle.

Gabrielle would do her damnedest to never see that "buckle" give way to complete collapse. She cared too much about the resort, her friendships and her craft to see that happen.

So she was okay with skipping the daybreak yoga class she shared with her friends and streamlining her beauty routine to make it to the Pearl two hours early. She even accepted with tremendous gusto that she'd need to not only substitute for an ill line cook, but also step in for a member of the waitstaff who'd been involved in a fender bender on Hollywood Boulevard. Dividing her morning between cooking and bopping into the dining room to take orders, tend to the breakfast buffet, refill coffee and mingle with guests had left tiny intervals for her to escape to the office and check in with her assistant.

Confronting the Pearl's main dining room, appreciating the quiet grandeur of its bold crystal touches; sharp, clean lines and tasteful blend of pure white against sleek gray, and realizing time had ticked to eleven thirty, she took a bracing breath. The bar was open. The restaurant's exceptional wine service was one of its famous features. The waitstaff was professionally trained in wine presentation and well versed in the Pearl's list, constantly educated through workshops and winery tours. But having been born to alcohol enthusiasts and expert wine collectors, Gabrielle remained the most knowledgeable, and guests often requested her personal recommendations—though she rarely could accommodate. Her schedule didn't normally allow it, and most who attempted to beckon her to their tables did so only because they thought the Pearl's top chef's attention was a sign of their celebrity, and that only annoyed the bejesus out of her.

Not in a mood to bolster the self-entitled's egos, she softened her features to *pleasant* and *approachable* and visited the buffet first. Smoothly, her staff was changing the offerings from European-influenced breakfast foods to afternoon-oriented selections ranging from fruit to salad options to an array of fresh breads.

"The air's so refreshing and cool in here, but the food stays just hot enough," a woman wrapped in pale chiffon said, pinching the buttered bread roll on her plate. "I spent the morning sorting out appointments and answering email in one of the cabanas at the pool, but the heat said it was time for a break. In here you wouldn't know it's a stifling California July out there."

My hair knows it. Gabrielle's gold-brushed auburn coils always seemed to know when heat and humidity were in cahoots. No scrunchie, barrette, bandanna or salon stylist's diligence could wrestle her curly hair to submission, so she'd finally embraced *expensively messy* as her style. Today she'd had to double up hairnets to secure it all out of the way, and now the loose curls lounged against her shoulders.

"The Pearl's committed to your comfort," Gabrielle told the woman, who accepted this with a smile. "Temperature distractions just won't do for us. We want you to concentrate on having a truly gourmet experience." For tourists, that usually meant eating in a relaxed environment. For locals concerned with being seen at *the* place to be seen, that often meant satisfying an impulse for superficial entertainment. For corporate types who convened here and spread papers and tablets on the tables and left room for little more than coffee trays, the frills the Pearl had to offer were only background novelties that couldn't compete with productivity.

"Well, now, friendly and respectful young ladies *aren't* extinct, after all. There's hope for America's youth yet." The woman eyed the Pearl's elegant logo in sapphire-blue on Gabrielle's self-customized asymmetrical T-shirt. Whether out of rebellion or simply because she couldn't help it, she hunted for creative ways to feed her greedy free spirit. "My grandniece is a college senior, has an internship in LA. What she wouldn't give to be in Belleza, working at a resort. Are you receiving college credit or a paycheck?"

It was Gabrielle's turn to smile. Another fact of life, much like her unruly curls, was that she appeared younger than her actual age. At fifteen she could pass for ten, at twenty she was mistaken as a middle school student, and at twenty-eight she was still being carded at nightclubs and invited to fraternity parties.

"A paycheck. My Harvard and Le Cordon Bleu days are far behind me." In her periphery, the Pearl's lead bartender was crooking two fingers. Continuing before the woman had an opportunity to flush with embarrassment, she said, "I'm Gabrielle Royce, executive chef here at the Pearl. Our bartender's waving me over, but I hope you'll enjoy your meal. Bring your grandniece sometime. The Belleza's holistic spa services are very popular with twentysomethings."

The bar was drawing a crowd quickly, but Jonah Grady—eighty-six in years, but ageless at heart—was a friend to the resort's owners, had been the town's favorite bachelor bartender since the place's conception and still commanded the space as though he were comfortably at home. In a way, this bar *was* his home. His companion, really, because no one in the Belleza Resort and Spa family could imagine them apart. They were fork and spoon, peanut butter and jelly, cheddar and cabaret sauvignon—a necessary pair.

Dressed in hues ranging from dove-white to slate, the bar gleamed gorgeously against sunlight. Soaring arched windows exposed palm trees as bold and proud as the resort itself and a watchful, slow-motion blue sky lounging over jagged mountains. The California sky was a sneaky thing. Lazy, unhurried and moody, it seemed to mock the people who hustled and bustled and hurried below it and most times appeared to move when no one was looking.

Gabrielle had a thing for sunrises and sunsets, but in recent weeks had found herself working through every dawn and dusk. When she wasn't at the restaurant, she was attending restaurant-related functions or carving out time to spend with her friends. Perhaps one evening she'd sit at the bar, let Jonah mix her a drink and talk about absolutely nothing important while the sky silently darkened to ink.

"Didn't mean to bother you," Jonah said once he set a glass of Chardonnay in front of an eager patron and walked to the end of the bar where Gabrielle waited. "Charlene accosted me in the staff lounge, begging me to let her work the bar for a while tonight. She said she'd cover my breaks."

"Our bartending team is solid." That was something to be thankful for, though she wished the same could be true for the kitchen and waitstaff. "Charlene knows this. Tell me you reminded her."

"I did." The youthful glint that Gabrielle thought she could always count on finding in the man's eyes now hinted at controlled frustration. "She stood in front of the bagel basket until I finally said I'd speak with you about it. There's ambition and then there's aggression. I don't like aggression."

"Okay, I'll get a minute with her," she said, but the glance he sent her was painfully abrasive. "Jonah, hey, I said I'll get a minute. I take food as seriously as the next person, and I swear Charlene won't hold the bagels hostage the next time she tries to vent about not wanting to be a hostess forever."

"It's not about taking food seriously. I take my job here seriously. I'm the head bartender and I don't need some bright-eyed girl trying to get her talons on my bar."

Damn. Jonah Grady was all old school charm and had *never* given off this degree of lethal anger. It was as though he were possessed—but to entertain that ridiculousness, she'd have to also believe in the other legends surrounding the resort. Curses and black magic and crappola like that. "So it's finally your turn to cave under the stress, hmm, Jonah? I assumed it'd be Robyn next, or maybe Kim's parents, but you're a mortal just like the rest of us."

"Don't go running to the Parkers and getting them on some campaign to have me retire. I'm still going strong. It's you young folks I'm thinking about. Friends bickering, people lying to the ones they say they care about, everyone hurting someone else to get ahead."

"If you're referring to what happened with Kim and Jaxon, that's all been ironed out," she said gently.

"It's all good now. They love each other, they're getting married and Robs and I support that."

"Another lie," he sneered. "Get as old as I am, you figure out that you've told enough lies to spot one a mile away. And Gabby, that was a damn pitiful one."

"What part of what I just said was a lie?" she demanded, her tone modulated and her gaze coasting down the bar to detect eavesdroppers.

"You support Kim and Jaxon? Wasn't long ago you were bouncing around here saying how you'd never do what she did."

"Which is true. I'd never screw a guest or fall in love with a guest, because it's too risky. Too complicated. Too easy to start to wonder whether my sexual relationships are being defined by business or if it's the other way around. Sex has nothing to do with my career, and it never will." She gulped in another bracing breath, because apparently the first one hadn't taken effect. "As far as Kim goes, what she has with Jaxon is real and, yeah, I support the hell out of that. I thought we were talking about Charlene anyway."

"The sooner you find her and her talons, the better."

"The 'talons' are acrylic nails and they're always tastefully manicured. Beautifully, actually. And she's not a girl. She's a young woman trying to make it in a town that's pretty much survival of the most ambitious. That *is* what she is—ambitious, not aggressive. She's part of Generation Me First. So am I, so I get it. Now quit acting like a crotchety old man and making me hang out in her corner. I'm mad at you for it."

"Let me pour you my best summer cocktail. I'll even give it some pizzazz, add a trick to it and get these folks worked up. You'll know I'm sorry."

"Thanks, Jonah," she said, reaching across the bar to pat his sleeve. No matter heat of summer or colliding tempers, he always portrayed an enviable fresh coolness while she was always packing prescription-strength deodorant and a miniature battery-powered fan. "But I can't drink now. I'm cooking and waitressing, and I'm not at a tasting."

"I know. I said it to gauge how riled up at me you were."

"You old badass," she whispered, stunned that he'd pulled something that was…oh, *precisely* what she might do in his position. "I need to get back to the kitchen, but don't forget you're going to owe me that drink."

Gabrielle surveyed the airy dining room as she picked up a near-empty carafe and brought it to the kitchen for a refill. Calmness. No…peacefulness. Peacefulness was good. You didn't mess with peacefulness.

She entered the kitchen and would never be able to explain why her focus darted past stainless steel counters and commercial appliances and rows of chefs and cooks to where Shoshanna was muscling an oversized stockpot off the top of a range. The flame leaped and swelled, and the woman turned in the direction of the prep sinks as a cart came fast around the corner preceded by a chef shouting, "Get that damn pot outta the way!"

Gabrielle ditched the carafe and rushed forward to try to stop the force of the cart, but a wheel popped off and the cart met Shoshanna in a vile collision. Dishes jerked off the cart and struck the floor in a dozen small crashes. The stockpot hit the sous-chef square in the middle and knocked her backward against the range. The flame reached for her, but failed to gain purchase, because a wave of boiling water had already escaped the pot and was bringing her down screaming onto the floor.

"Lift her off the friggin' water!" Gabrielle shouted above the chaotic gasps and curses. So many intelligent, ingenious minds, yet those who'd actually paused in their tasks only gathered about loosely to watch in paralyzed shock as Shoshanna writhed in heart-shredding pain.

"Oh, my God! Damn it, my God, she was boiling that at one-thirty Fahrenheit," a line cook said, as the man beside him shook his head and grumbled "I can't watch this" and went back on the line.

This was *her* staff? Sure, she preached that the Pearl couldn't stop, but a horrendous scalding was a genuine emergency. She began to reach for the woman, but a booming voice and hulking body cut her off.

"Chef Royce, protect your hands," Stu said. Ready with towels, he scooped up Shoshanna and the puddle of steaming water nearly turned Gabrielle's stomach.

"She's been in it about twenty seconds," she said, watching him carry the sous-chef to vacant floor space near a prep table. *Third degree. There has to be third degree somewhere.* "Did anyone call 911? *Somebody* call 911, now. At one-thirty, she was rolling in it too long."

"We don't know that yet," he said, peeling off Shoshanna's apron, and Gabrielle knelt to help unbutton the drenched shirt. If the fabric stuck, they'd need to leave it be and send up a prayer for her. "We know she's hurting like hell and needs to cool down."

Nicola appeared with a bucket of cold water. "And what about her leg? What do we know about that, besides the human tibia isn't made to bend?"

Oh, Lord. A break.

Shoshanna's wails drummed against Gabrielle's ears, but they were able to remove her soggy shirt and cool her skin continuously until paramedics arrived at the kitchen's private exit. A strip on her forearm had begun to blister, and Gabrielle hoped that area was the worst of her burns. Her abdomen and a spot on her neck were beet-red. The scald injuries combined with the obviously broken shin meant she wouldn't be returning to this kitchen anytime soon and the Pearl would need to recruit an immediate replacement.

An hour later, the kitchen was still strained and in crisis mode. Gabrielle had reported the incident to the Belleza's general manager—finding it crazy-difficult to converse with Kim as an employee to her employer rather than as friends—and was now struggling to shoulder Shoshanna's duties on top of the extras she'd already taken on.

"Charlene," she said, approaching the posh hostess desk. Charlene Vincent's perfected breezy, old-fashioned Hollywood glam look belied the day's insanity. Whether it was her hairstyle or the color scheme of her makeup or the figure-amplifying dress, Gabrielle couldn't pinpoint, but the woman was a replica of Marilyn Monroe in *Some Like It Hot.* "Shoshanna Smirnov's out of commission."

"Oh, I heard. So sad. Really sad." Charlene's pouty smile remained in place, and when she noticed the irked frown Gabrielle couldn't hide, she explained, "The hostess is the face of a restaurant. I'm the front door of the Pearl. Got to greet the guests with a great smile. But, really, *so* sad about Shosh."

"With her gone, we're even more severely short-staffed than we were this morning. I'm putting one of the bartenders here at the desk, and I'd like you to wait tables for the rest of your shift. It'd free me up a bit to stay in the kitchen."

"Oh… I totally understand you. Yeah, if I were so sweaty and couldn't go freshen up, I'd want to be un-seen, too. So many A-list guys are out to play. A girl can't get any decent action if she doesn't put her best face forward."

Gabrielle felt her eyes narrow. *Jonah, I can't believe you provoked me to defend this person.* "I need to stay in the kitchen to *cook,* Charlene."

The hostess's smile faltered. "Can't do it, sorry, Gabs. I'm not dressed to be rushing back and forth and I'd never get grease stink out of this dress. But I guess tomorrow I could help you out. Who can I speak to about upping my salary?"

"There's no salary upping, *Char.* We're all pulling together because the Pearl functions as one unit. Think about that before you come back tomorrow. And if you want to be put at the bar, you're gonna really want to absorb what I'm telling you instead of cornering some-one who, even if he wanted to train you, lacks the au-thority to change your position at this restaurant."

"Anything else?" Charlene said tightly. "I'm due to go on break."

Yes. Quit flirting with every guy who walks in here wearing a suit and Rolex. Think about how you're com-ing off to other people. Change your attitude.

No way. Gabrielle had no right to dictate to this

woman the same jazz that her mother had dictated to her before Gabrielle had removed herself from the Royce family fold to design her own life. Defying her family, choosing culinary arts over med school, hadn't been painless, and she'd be damned if she shook her finger at someone who had the prerogative to live outside the lines as much as she wanted without shattering laws and stomping company rules.

"Nothing else, Charlene. I'll get someone from bartending to hold down the desk while you're on break."

"Good. After work I'm getting one of those quickie facials. There's a party in LA my friends are hyped about, and today's been *so* stressful that I might check it out to Zen things down a bit." Charlene dismissed her with a head tilt and a sharp wave goodbye.

Returning to the kitchen, Gabrielle was thinking very unpleasant things about self-*un*conscious, self-*un*aware folks when she realized the doors hadn't swung closed behind her.

Turning so suddenly that her pink Converse hightops squeaked, she stopped just as abruptly when her gaze latched on to the man in front of her and… Would. Not. Let. Go.

It wasn't that she recognized him, exactly. He had to be a stranger, because the arousal that had her feeling kind of weak and had turned her erogenous zones against her and had taunted that she'd better add "change panties" to her to-do list was unfamiliar and a little bit disturbing.

No words had passed between them, and although she was sure she'd never met him before Gabrielle wanted this man and everything his angry mouth, marble-hard body and large hands could do for her.

The hands. They were good hands. Not pretty—she didn't get hot for men whose hands were prettier than her scarred chef's hands. This guy's were closer to ugly, actually. Ugly but clean. Mmm, she *so* liked that. They were splayed against the doors, holding them open wide, and every masculine line from fingertip to wrist seduced her to immediately imagine how deep her mouth could take those long, big-knuckled fingers.

Did he know what her mind was sketching? Was he standing in her doorway in his six-figure suit and watching her through his five-figure sunglasses and seeing sex and nakedness and freaky things that high-society debutantes from upstate New York weren't sup-posed to know? Had he figured out in seconds that if he asked, she might let him strum her, work her and pleasure her?

She really hoped not. The man didn't belong in the Pearl's kitchen or Gabrielle's unfiltered thoughts. As certain as she was of her attraction to him, she knew he was a guest. That made him out of reach, even though she could stretch out a hand and stroke a path from his neck to his sleek leather belt that she was confident she could find a few raunchy uses for.

"Can I do you?" Gabrielle's brain tripped over itself. Okay, *what*? "Can I do something for you?"

"You *could've* come to my table when I signaled you, but, since you went ahead talking to that host-ess and walked right past me again, I figured the only way to get the food I ordered was if I took it from the kitchen myself, so you might as well just give me the damn plate."

And now we return to lifestyles of the rich and self-important. "I apologize."

"For neglecting a patron? That apology's late and useless, but I'll take it."

Gabrielle's jaw almost hit the toes of her Converse high-tops. "Excuse me, but not seeing you isn't the same as neglect." Asshole. Wait, she didn't *say* that aloud, did she? He didn't wear that struck, stunned expression that assholes usually wore when told that they were assholes, so she was safe. Well, as safe as she could be staring down a man who was as sexy as he was domineering. "The Pearl doesn't take orders and refuse to fulfill them as a practice. I'm not sure where your waiter or waitress could've gone."

"Waiter. He took my order and disappeared. Your superiors might want to get control of their staff."

"Bear with us. We're recovering from unusual circumstances right now."

"Look, I didn't order my Cobb salad with a side of PR doublespeak. Can I get the plate or do I get in my ride and find somewhere else to go for lunch?"

"I've already apologized, so I'm not going to again. But what I told you isn't 'PR doublespeak.' It's true that this restaurant doesn't normally see one of its best international chefs taken away in an ambulance with scald burns and a broken leg." Gabrielle ignored the swift change in his disposition, which made him as hot and mesmerizing as a flame. She had better command of the sense she was born with when she wasn't thinking dirty things about this man's jaw and goatee and rude mouth. "If you'd like to repeat your order, I'll personally bring it to your table along with a complimentary wine."

"Cobb salad, no eggs, blue cheese dressing on the side."

"Might I suggest sauvignon blanc? The bouquet is an excellent complement to the garden flavors in your meal."

"Sauvignon blanc," he conceded, stepping back and letting the doors finally close.

"You're cute when you're all pissed off and horny." Even when Gabrielle spun and pretended to upper-cut him, Stu didn't relent. "What are you going to do about that?"

"Fix what he ordered."

"No, *I'll* prepare the Cobb salad. You blot your face, gloss that luscious mouth of yours and get the blanc."

"He's a guest, Chef Merritt."

"Who's also sexy. You heard what Chef Smirnov said earlier. If he turns out to be eligible, you have a decision to make." Stu leaned toward her ear, thumping back her curls. "In case you make the *wrong* decision, take a break and hose yourself down before your pheromones start throwing everyone off."

Chapter 2

If a man can't trust himself, he's screwed.

Geoffrey Girard's philosophy had hauled him through some rough times, taught him to never question his instincts and maneuvers and had been all the reason in the world to never lie to himself. That was *before* he'd swaggered into the Pearl and had a faceoff with that smokin'-fine smartass waitress.

Now his philosophy was a handful of empty words strung together that didn't mean anything concrete. He wasn't confident in his decision to stay at this restaurant and wait for her to come to him. And, damned straight, he was lying to himself when he silently said he could accept his meal and walk away without wanting to claim what wasn't on some fancy silver menu.

Returning to his private table in front of an arched window exposing a complicated-looking abstract water feature and mountains that stabbed the afternoon sky, he tried to convince himself that the reason he hadn't taken his Bugatti Veyron from the valet and put the Belleza and all its hedonistic luxuries in the rearview mirror was because he was owed the meal he'd spent valuable time ordering and to prove to this restaurant—from the waitress to the corporates signing her checks—that *no one* ignored him without regretting it.

She'd said she hadn't seen him wave from his table, but he didn't trust that.

She had been in perfect view, crossing through the dining room with a leap in her step that made all that curly hair bounce in rhythm with her breasts. In a white top and black bottoms, she matched the other servers—except, she didn't exactly. The shirt was cut at a slanted angle, the pants were smooth, tight leather and on her feet were pink Chuck Taylor high-tops. Quirk or kink, he couldn't call it, but underlying that mismatched creative strangeness was something high maintenance about her. She was art, a piece that was too expensive and something you didn't understand, but you had to have it anyway.

Cutting past him, she'd chatted it up with that hostess, the hot blonde who'd earlier brushed her fingers over his Bulgari wristwatch and handed him a business card that read Charlene Vincent, Model, Actress & Voice Talent. Her nails had been painted to look like starry skies, and she'd appraised him with sex and opportunity in her eyes. He'd taken the card but wouldn't be taking hot Charlene up on what she was offering. And if she and the waitress were tight enough to be whispering secrets at the hostess station, then he didn't need to be sitting at this table tensed up with a semi for either one of them.

Plenty of women had reddish-gold curls that he could fall asleep counting. Skin the color of the palest caramel couldn't be *that* damned hard to find. And she couldn't be the only woman in this town who was working with all her original parts. Hell, could be she was saving up her tips for some surgical enhancements. God knew he'd been with too many LA groupies and Beverly Hills hotties who thought fake tits and toxin injections and bolts of weave were requisites to getting ahead.

Maybe that was what had him all jacked up in the head today. He was done with the monotony of fakeness and deception tattooed on the R&B world and was getting all hard up because he thought that a waitress with wild hair, a soft-looking ass and an outfit that didn't make all that much sense might show him a way out.

Geoffrey would really be lying to himself if he tried to believe he wanted out of R&B. He moved around in that realm like a god, had built his empire from the ground up and it had saved him from the ghetto he'd been born into. But once in a while a man had a taste for something real, and invading this restaurant's kitchen, he thought he'd found it in a waitress.

It would do him good to take his food and leave, and hand off the rest of his dealings with the Belleza to any of his assistants. He paid them for more than discretion and schedule managing, didn't he?

He set his smartphone on the table. Everything from the tablecloth to the long-stemmed flowers standing at attention in a crystal centerpiece was crisp and pristine—

no doubt masterminded by a perfectionist with an obsession for symmetry and a control complex.

Not that he was hatin' on them—after all, he was the same way.

And that was why he didn't get further than fingerprint-unlocking his phone. He wouldn't be passing tomorrow's meeting with the Belleza's big-hype master chef off to one of his assistants. The celebration honoring Phenom Jones, G&G Records's record-shattering artist who'd just hit platinum, was Geoffrey's project. He was a wanted man, on clubs' VIP lists and in front of paparazzi's cameras and in high-priced gold diggers' dreams, but he carved out time for the people whose talent, charisma and perseverance made his company money in a brutal-as-hell industry.

Coming here on another client's recommendation, he'd intended to spend a few days at the resort and form his own perception. No honest man with an appetite for the hottest of luxuries could deny the Belleza's appeal, but so far the only thing that had impressed him about the Pearl was its competence in recruiting sexy women.

Speaking of sexy…

The waitress closed in on his table, carrying a bottle of wine and a tray heavy enough to accentuate her delicate biceps. Regarding her with appreciation, he got a frown in return. And he didn't like that he deserved that frown and every profane word behind it.

"We can't start over?"

"And pretend you didn't barge into that kitchen like some lord-of-everything invading enemy territory?" A bubble of silence followed, giving her a chance to frown again and him ample time to come to the conclusion that hell, no, they couldn't start over. She pierced the bubble with, "Cobb salad, no eggs, blue cheese dressing on the side, and sauvignon blanc. May I?"

Nodding, he let her uncover the food, then she presented the chilled wine with the kind of animation and knowledge that could fool anyone into thinking she had years of experience indulging in vineyards all over the world. Her delivery was professional, her words intelligent and her attitude confident. Another point for the Pearl, then. The place knew how to train its people.

When she poured and started to step away, he pointed to the opposite gray chair. "Take a seat. Please?"

"How is it that you made a perfectly polite word sound like a warning?"

The corner of Geoffrey's mouth rose. *"Please,"* he said again, softer, thinking he'd like nothing more than to watch the word drift from her supple mouth. "Was that better?"

Lazily, she blinked at him, and a deep hint of color surfaced on her cheeks and down the line of her neck. Continuing on that trajectory, he saw that her shirt was stretched tight over a pair of beaded nipples. She was aroused, for him, and he couldn't let her leave now.

"I want you to taste it first." Geoffrey pointed to the chair again. "And then there's something I need to say."

"Sitting with guests and drinking isn't something I normally do on shift," she said, her focus darting between the chair and the direction of the kitchen. People clustered around the tables and wait staff wheeled about the place taking orders, delivering entrées and plucking tips. "Do you think you'd like a different wine?"

"If you're really interested in finding out what I'd

like," he said, sitting back against his chair, "take a seat and I'll tell you."

Another hesitant beat passed before she slid into the vacant chair. Something was different about her. Her mouth. She'd put on makeup, and those satiny pink lips tantalized him as they hovered over his wineglass.

Lucky friggin' wineglass.

"Fantastic aroma. My senses are really open to the oak."

With a pleased little nod, she said, "I'll get you a fresh glass."

"This one's good," he interrupted, taking it. The fruit flavors were dominant but the oak held its own. "Is your chef going to be all right?"

"Shoshanna Smirnov. The Pearl's best sous-chef. 'All right' is hard to say. The medical center reported second- and third-degree burns, and a broken leg. A cart lost a wheel and came down on her while she was carrying a pot of boiling water. Freak accident, if you buy into that as an explanation." She sighed. "I'm worried about her. She's my friend."

"Close staff, for chefs and waitresses to be friends," he commented.

"Friendships don't make this restaurant a success. There's a huge cast of personalities behind the scenes— we don't always get along and there are occasions when not everyone pulls their weight. What we have is a common interest in providing an incomparable dining experience to each of our guests."

"Yeah, arguing with kitchen staff was something I'd never experienced, so thanks for that."

She laughed, and the sound seemed to grab him

and hold him still. So beautiful. Man, if he could get her to laugh again…

Before he could attempt it, her expression retreated to guarded.

"I wanted to say I'm sorry for speaking to you the way I did before," he said. "Freak accidents, mixed-up orders and folks not pulling their weight, that comes from the top. Management. Subpar management isn't *your* fault." A crooked eyebrow answered him. "Look, food service is a stressful business as it is without people treating your space like—what'd you call it?— enemy territory."

"Can I ask what you'd know about food service?"

"I bused tables in college, for a work-study program."

"Work-study?"

"Yeah." He considered her. The small frame and girlish way she strutted around the restaurant might deceive some at first, but the woman in front of him was an expert wine presenter and watched him with eyes that shone with blunt wisdom, not naiveté. "I'm living in Beverly Hills and driving sports cars now, but I came from the other side. I know there are folks praying for miracles and turning to crime to survive another day. When you've got a chance to make something better for yourself, through college work-study or waiting tables at a resort, you'll put up with anything to hang on to it. So what I'm saying is, I understand what this gig means to you and I'm thinking you got the skills to make something solid out of this. And I want to thank you for handling our…run-in…with professionalism even when I didn't. Don't have to believe me, but my mama would've put a hand upside my head for talking to you that way."

"Mine would lecture me for talking back to a man." Her brown eyes bolted open, and he detected a confidence she hadn't meant to share. "What I should say is some people wouldn't find it very professional of me to strike back like that. But that's how fighting works—swing at me and I'll swing back."

"I wasn't trying to pick a fight," he said, starting in on the salad.

"I wasn't trying to finish one." She shrugged. "So here we are."

"I like where we are right now. I think you do, too."

Conflict rode her features, but she sat there mutely until another female voice levitated over the hubbub around them. A svelte African American woman had her finger in a waiter's face. Talking fast, the only word she insisted on emphasizing was *endives*.

"My intervention's needed at that table."

"Shouldn't management get involved?"

Pausing as if to explain something, she appeared to change tracks. "I know her. Trina Erickson. If anyone at the Pearl can handle her malfunction, it's me."

Maybe the guy *wasn't* an asshole.

After dealing with produce drama, courtesy of Trina Erickson, who'd been doubling as a friend and an enemy since Merriweather Academy in Massachusetts, Gabrielle had admittedly been excited to revisit the man who'd irked her with his rudeness then had charmed her stupid.

If snapping at a guest was unprofessional in her book, then what would she call keeping him company at his table, sharing his wine and feeling her undies become moister by the moment? Oh, yup, stupid.

Anyone could have come upon them and misconstrued the situation. Or, worse, gotten the situation exactly right. The Pearl's executive chef had been hot, bothered and unable to clearly think beyond the erotic demand drumming through her system. In a crazy way Trina's endive crisis had been just the interruption Gabrielle needed to break away and regroup.

But at some point during the bustle of tending to her former classmate's produce dilemma, giving the hot stranger his check and offering Trina's waiter a few encouraging words, Gabrielle had started to feel mighty craptastic for allowing the guest to assume she was a waitress. She hadn't gone out of her way to *lie,* but she'd allowed him to veer onto the wrong path when it came to her role at the Pearl—and that wasn't good business.

Choosing to rectify things, she'd circled around to his table to find his chair empty and the leather check presenter stuffed with cash to cover his meal plus a tip in the form of a crisp-enough-to-slice-you C-note.

Gripping the check presenter, Gabrielle stared at the wineglass they'd shared and found the faint press of her lip gloss there.

You naughty, naughty chef. Quit cooking up scandal.

They hadn't exchanged names. She supposed she could ask Charlene if she'd gotten details, but the hostess would angle a way to benefit from sharing any info. But if she were being practical—and even a free spirit needed to be practical sometimes—she shouldn't care too much. More important than attraction was the reality that he was forbidden real estate.

That condom Gabrielle had been carrying in her

compact mirror since spring might linger through summer, but at least she wouldn't end up a hypocrite for a little dirty fraternizing with a Belleza guest.

As the bussers arrived at the table, she went to the register then stuffed the one-hundred-dollar tip into an apothecary jar in the kitchen. The kitchen and serving staff voluntarily added money to the jar, and each month the funds were donated to a Los Angeles homeless shelter.

"Swing and a miss?" Stu asked as she washed her hands at the scrub sink.

"I wouldn't say I even picked up the bat." Gabrielle tossed her head. "It's all right. *Que sera, sera.*"

"You're breaking my heart."

"I'm not." She smiled. "You're as bad as Robyn and Kim. Except you just want me taken so I don't go tagging along with you to all of LA's hotspots."

"That's not true, Chef Royce." Stu's blue eyes rolled. "No, okay, it is true. But you have to lift your head up one day and see that your career won't vanish if you go on a date off the clock. One night, just put on something slutty and have a good time."

"Or *not* put on something slutty, and have a good time anyway?"

"Brilliant."

After taking a break to call the Belleza Medical Center to check up on Shoshanna and then to visit Kimberly Parker's office for a much-needed friend-to-friend talk that had remained locked on Shoshanna's incident and all the other recent spookiness, Gabrielle worked in the kitchen through the dinner rush. In recent weeks it had shifted to seven to nine. It was after ten-thirty when she took her jacket and purse and left the Pearl for the night.

Yawning, she opened the door to the stylish home-magazine condo that housed several members of the resort's top employees. The place had amenities and luxuries her most fanciful dreams hadn't imagined, and a view that for a good week had poked the sensitive side of her that cried over wonders like haunting fiction, bigheaded kittens and California dawns. Her neighbors were her two best friends. No hassled staff or overindulged celebrities could invade this space.

So she ought to be deliriously happy to turn on the lights, break out her favorite shower gel, wash the day away…and pass out cold at eleven o'clock on a balmy summer night.

Tomorrow she was expected to work a half day, as she was preparing a menu for a potential new client. At one o'clock she'd be meeting with him. An R&B mogul, her assistants had told her. A music producer. Jeffrey *something*. She tried to recall the name, but her brain was still poached. After some rest and perhaps a nice woodsy wine, she'd be on all cylinders again.

Showered and snuggled-up on the custom-designed upholstered sofa, her face peeking out from beneath a pillow just so she could clearly hear Guns N' Roses on her Bluetooth speaker, she was fidgety.

"I'm exhausted but I can't rest, and keyed up but I can't do anything about it." Gabrielle shoved the pillow aside and rolled off the sofa. Staring up at the leisurely whir of the Tahitian-style ceiling fan, she decided that in limbo was a hell of an awful place to be. Love had hit close to home, and soon Kimberly would be marrying a man who was meant for her in every conceivable way. Then Cupid would probably come a knockin' on Robyn's door. And that would leave Gabrielle left with the Pearl and a serious bout of happy-ever-after envy.

"Wrong," she muttered. "I *can* do something about it." She got to her feet and consulted her closet. Her lingerie armoire was seriously lacking in actual lingerie. In fact, there were a lot of socks—and quick inventory said about half had mates that had disappeared in the wash.

Tonight she'd visit an after-hours adults-only boutique and revamp her undies collection with what made her feel sexy and confident. Tomorrow, no one but Gabrielle would know she was business on top and party underneath, and when she sat down with the record producer she would rock the meeting and celebrate with a good time in LA and a guy who might just help her forget the stranger who'd signed himself up for her fantasies when he'd barged into her kitchen and switched on her libido.

Grabbing her keys, Gabrielle congratulated herself on a plan well schemed. When you had a great plan, what could go wrong?

Confirm concert venues. Turn around contracts to his legal group. Ensure that his assistants toured his hot springs studio retreat and had it prepared for next week's VIP-guests-only recording session weekend party. Those were only a few of the demands that Geoffrey could be confronting this morning. Each item was important and tried to seduce his attention, but in the end nothing had deterred him from taking the Bugatti Veyron out early to drive from his cottage suite rental to the Pearl.

In steel-colored Armani and prepared with notes loaded onto his smartphone, Geoffrey arrived over an hour before his meeting with the restaurant's executive chef, and it wasn't because menu pitches and plays for his business got him excited.

He was here because he wanted another look at the waitress from yesterday. No, what he wanted was a conversation with her outside the restaurant, on neutral grounds where she wouldn't feel the need to dart her gaze left and right every few seconds to see if someone would catch her at his table.

The woman was natural, inside and out. Real.

In his universe, real women were rare and real connections were things only idiots put stock in. He lived sagely, dating women who agreed to sex and a few enlightening conversations. He didn't commit himself to complex relationships that would only fall apart on a damned gossip site's homepage. The predictability of his hookups was a double-sided coin: good because he always knew what to expect, and bad because there was no adventure in saying hello, tapping it, saying goodbye and repeating with someone new when the next urge hit.

"It's under your skin, isn't it?" a velvety voice said. The bombshell hostess. "The Pearl, of course. It must be under your skin now, because you're back so soon."

"Hey… Charlene, is it?"

"Mmm-hmm," she whispered, stepping around her desk to lean enticingly against it. "Very few things, sir, are more flattering to a woman than when an attractive, accomplished man remembers her name."

"I'm looking for someone," he said. Charlene had the kind of body a brother could write songs about and her forwardness was hot as hell, but he didn't see the gain in forcing attraction that didn't exist. "A waitress. Curly-haired, slender, short…"

He almost said *pretty*, but that would've been a generic lie. The woman wasn't pretty; she was addictive.

"You mean Gabby." With a shrug, Charlene rounded the desk. "She's got a meeting later today, but knowing her she'll still come in early to crack the whip. I can sit you at a table if you want to wait. And meanwhile, I can keep you entertained—"

Geoffrey intercepted the proposition. "Doesn't a woman find it flattering when a guy she gives her number to follows through with calling her?"

Obviously remembering that she'd circled her phone number and handed him her business card yesterday, Charlene swallowed and stared back at him.

"If I'd wanted to flatter you like that," he continued, firmly enough to infiltrate her agenda, "if I'd wanted you, Charlene, I would've called you."

Leaving her at the desk to glower and grumble words he hadn't heard since his last high-roller poker game in the Hills, he selected his own table and waited for the waitress. He was there, leaning forward on his chair, his fingers steepled, when she came up to him in a black short-sleeved jacket secured with a ribbon over a thin white top and white jeans. The leopard print high heels gave her a few borrowed inches of height, but when he stood up, he still had an easy foot on her.

Yesterday he'd worn sunglasses. Today it was her turn. Would she take them off if he asked, so they could look at each other naked eye to naked eye?

"The hostess said your name's Gabby."

She nodded. "Can I help you?"

"Oh, it's 'can I *help* you' today," he said, referencing the blunder she'd probably assumed he hadn't noticed the afternoon before.

Can I do you? Yeah, that had stayed with him all last night and his unspoken answer still hadn't changed. *Absolutely. After I do you.*

"Th-that was an error. A really unfortunate error."

"Freudian slip."

"Did you come back to the Pearl for an apology for that, too?"

Geoffrey held up his open hands. "I'm here in peace. And the hope that you'll let me take you away from here for a cup of coffee."

"The Pearl has fantastic coffee."

"The Pearl has dozens of folks all up in your business, and I'd like to get some more time with you."

Gabby shook her head. "I'm not leaving the resort, so no. I have a can't-miss meeting shortly and don't want to take a chance on getting caught in a traffic clog. Sorry…but I need to ask, why me?"

"Because of yesterday. You didn't look at me and start picturing how you'd spend my money."

"No, that's not me. I looked at you and saw a man who's alpha and arrogant. In my head I called you another word that starts with the letter *A*, but I probably should leave it at that."

Geoffrey laughed, and it garnered swiveling heads and prying murmurs.

"Shh!" As she raised a fingertip to her lips, he caught her hand and kissed that finger.

"Gabby…if you have coffee with me, there's a chance I'll kiss you again."

Wiggling her hand free of his grasp, she said, "Kiss me again and people are going to start talking."

"Then let's go someplace where they're not watching." Geoffrey was all good with letting her lead him out of the Pearl and to an elevator that brought them to the third floor. Their destination was a balcony lined with plants. Just before the balcony was an intimate room that housed vending machines—one being a self-serve espresso machine.

"You said coffee," she reminded him, plucking two foam cups. "This is where staff occasionally go for self-sentenced timeouts."

Vending machine espresso in hand, they went to the balcony.

"We can say nothing at all, or figure out what we're doing here," she finally said. "Either way, we can't be making this into some routine."

"Since I walked out of the restaurant yesterday, it's been nothing but you. In my head, all night, and I can't change it. I'm chained here."

Gabby swallowed a mouthful of espresso with a strangled little gulp. "Oh… That, what you're saying, you *can't* think about me that way."

"Why not? Tell me, and make me understand, then."

"Because I work for this resort. I'm an employee."

"I don't care that you're a waitress."

"No? Do you care that I'm not a waitress?" She led Geoffrey to the balcony, which was empty of staff or guests. Setting her cup on a nearby table, she took off her sunglasses and looked him square in the eye. "Because I'm not. I'm the Pearl's executive chef."

Executive chef? Aw, damn it. "Chef…uh… Gabrielle Royce?"

"Yes. Curly-haired, short and slender." She shrugged a shoulder and revolved on her leopard heels to stroke a robust verdant leaf. "The hostess found it imperative to divulge the 'unflattering' way you described me to her."

"You think that's unflattering?"

"No. I'm each of those things, and proud to be."

"I could've added *sexy* and *smartass*, but then that might've made our meeting more awkward than it's already going to be." Geoffrey set his coffee down, went to her and gently turned her to face him. She was yielding but still challenging...was giving off all kinds of heat, but still harbored cold uncertainty. Extending his hand to hers, he murmured against her feathery smooth curls, "Geoffrey Girard, G&G Records. Your one o'clock's with me."

Chapter 3

The man whose face infiltrated her thoughts last night and whose hands touched her in her early morning dreams was Geoffrey Girard, the account she was supposed to win for the Belleza? It had to be a cosmic joke—or, more realistically, a test. Robyn might not have the motive, but Kim had the savvy to challenge Gabrielle's convictions.

Place an intriguing stranger in Gabrielle's path, then have him reveal himself as a big shot client who'd tempt her beyond all common sense and expose her for the hypocrite she was. Not that she could blame her friend for it. After the way she'd blatantly taken on some holier than thou attitude toward Kimberly's relationship with Jaxon, she rationalized that a bit of clever retaliation was justifiable.

Justifiable, but not effective. Gabrielle hadn't crossed

the line—yet. She was on the line with this man, so close to crossing it. In fact, if she let him come any closer, the heat swirling between them might burn the line to ash and there'd be no saving herself. "So did you owe Kim Parker a favor?"

A confused squint was all he gave her.

Oh, my stars. He's gorgeous as hell when he frowns.

"I'm a good sport when it comes to pranks, but this is a little much," she went on, though she'd give her friend points for creativity and execution. Geoffrey was every undefined detail she wanted in a man. And he was supremely off-limits.

"I don't owe anyone a favor, and I've never met Kim Parker. But I want to know why she'd want to prank you and how I could be involved in that."

"Oh." So it *was* a cosmic joke. "Kimberly's my friend and the gist of a very complicated story is that I recently began to realize how extremely wrong I was about something, and I thought Kimberly had put us together to show me the error of my ways, I guess."

"I wouldn't see you as someone who often admits she's wrong."

"That's because I'm not often wrong."

Geoffrey started to smile and something began to shake loose inside her. Control. It was failing her, but thank God she caught herself in time to get a grip on her senses. Always in tune with herself, Gabrielle could blame no one for her choices. She was her own true best friend. No one could ever know her better than she knew herself. She wouldn't let a man with a startlingly fascinating smile change that.

"But when I *am* wrong," she added, "I admit it."

He continued watching her.

"Well, eventually." She would've shrugged if he'd given her enough room. Instead he had her framed in, with leaves hugging her and his scent stroking her from all angles. That the man didn't overdo it on the cologne was a plus.

Wait—what was she doing? She shouldn't be giving him pluses now that she knew he was even more than a Belleza guest. She should be searching him for flaws. The alpha attitude aside, he wasn't perfect and she'd be setting herself up for doom to start thinking he was.

Flaw, she thought. *Find a flaw.*

The hands. He had intimidating, ugly hands. Except they were sexy and this morning in the shower she started to think her loofah was prepping her skin for his touch. Recognizing the thought as completely silly, she'd doubted she'd even see him again and had been shocked to her leopard-print Manolo Blahnik pumps to find him waiting for her at the Pearl.

"What you asked me yesterday, about starting over," she said. "I'm thinking now would be a great time to give that a try."

"If we started over, the attraction would still be here."

"Attraction's not good for business."

"Pretending it's not here…what's that good for?" he challenged.

"I don't know. In addition to being wrong on occasion, I also on even rarer occasions am totally without an answer. I don't know what to do with…" She would not say *attraction.* Saying it would give it more dimension, a degree of realness she wasn't equipped to handle.

"With what?" he said.

"Wanting you." Oh, no. *Attraction* would've been a tamer option, compared to blunt *wanting you.* "I…"

"You want me, Gabby?"

"Gabrielle. Not Gabby."

"Okay. You want me, Gabrielle?"

"I—" She twisted away from him. "I think we should talk about our professional dilemma. You're Geoffrey Girard and until you realized that I'm the executive chef you were considering naming this resort as the venue for your event."

"I didn't say I'm no longer considering the Belleza. A client of mine stayed here last month. Cole. He recommended this place."

Demanding, tough-to-please Cole had recommended the resort? The singer had been an especially difficult guest, but he had a way of getting past a person's defenses and was an okay man. That he was sending the Belleza new elite business made him a *very* okay man.

"I talked to your assistant," Geoffrey said.

"Roarke." The office manager from heaven. Roarke was steady, a paperwork genius and a people whisperer. If he wasn't dating his own heaven-sent angel, she could see herself electing him to be her better half.

"Then I had a talk with the lead event planner—"

"That'd be Robyn. She's my friend, as well."

"We discussed some options for the party. No pranks came up in the conversation, I swear."

Laughing, she was relieved. Somehow, knowing her friends weren't out to catch her sexing up a guest made her feel safe about enjoying him in private like this. Yes, she was setting herself up for trouble, but as long as she realized it she could control how far things went and how much trouble she invited. "Maybe the hookup rules are lax in the music biz, but at this resort staff and guests don't get personal. It's just not a common practice."

"Common, meaning it *does* happen, though."

"Yes, but not for me. I have to be honest, okay? I want you, and that's personal and chances are it's an extraordinarily bad idea. But I want your business more. I want your account for the Belleza."

"If I chose another venue, what would that mean for us?"

"I can't entertain that, Geoffrey. I'm sorry, but this has to be about business. It needs to be about me showing you why you should choose the Belleza to host this party. Let me show you my vision. Let me show you why it'd be a mistake to choose another venue."

"Okay."

"Okay?" No debate, no pressure, no persuasion?

"Yeah. Okay." He went to the high-backed chairs surrounding the table. Sitting, he relaxed his form, stretched his long legs out in front of him.

"Everything's in my office," she said. "My assistant's there. We have a presentation prepared. 3D graphics."

"We can hold our next meeting in your office, Gabrielle. We're already here and I'd rather listen to you talk." He gestured to the seat beside him, so she took the one across. "Hey, how's your friend? The chef who had the accident yesterday?"

"She's not in life-threatening danger. There's a small-scale third-degree burn, a broken bone." *Damaged* would've been more accurate. She'd visited Shoshanna this morning to find her vibrant friend broken beyond the snapped tibia now set in a cast. Bandaged and emotionally wrecked, Shoshanna lay crying soundlessly and Gabrielle had to prod her to confess that she was worried about being permanently replaced as sous-chef. Gabrielle had already made up her mind that a replacement would be only temporary—but after sitting with Shoshanna she intended to make sure she, Kimberly and HR were all on the same page and had their loyal and talented sous-chef's position waiting for her to resume once her injuries healed.

"Roarke told me you were set on an after-dark party, but I'd like to present the option of taking advantage of the slow sunset. Get things rolling earlier in the evening and you'll see that a sunset backdrop will heighten the atmosphere. If you prefer a more temp-controlled location, the Pearl's dining room is a fabulous choice. We'd reserve the entire space and transform it to suit the theme we agree on. There are also a couple of premiere outdoor spots on the property that offer spectacular views of the sun dropping over the mountains. Think about it. Drinking a glass of—what do you like? Scotch? Brandy? Vodka?"

"No preference," he said, and though his voice was strangely tight, she didn't let it slow her down.

"Drinking a glass of brandy, the mood relaxed yet elegant, the background splendid but not intrusive. The sun slowly melts behind the mountaintops, quietly telling you that the night belongs to you now. It belongs to your guests and your celebration. What do you think?"

"I think I want to take the time to watch the sun set tonight."

"Do it. Of course I'll be jealous that you'd have the time."

"If I asked you to watch it with me, you'd say you don't have the time?"

"Afraid I don't. I'm on shift tonight. Closing again. But you watch it, and imagine what it'd be like to share that kind of wonder with your guests."

"Or I'd imagine sharing it with you."

Gabrielle crossed her legs, leisurely swinging her foot to disguise the giddyup of her hormones. The man was so single-minded, had laser focus and had it trained on turning her into happy, hot putty. "Is this your roundabout way of adding me to your guest list? Because as chef in charge, I'd be there anyway. As would my assistant, Roarke."

"You keep mentioning Roarke."

"Because he's my assistant. He's worth mentioning."

"Is he also your bodyguard? More than that, even?"

"He's my *assistant*. Nothing more. Just as you'd be my client and nothing more. It's the cleanest way to do business, across the board."

Geoffrey leaned forward and her foot stopped moving. She stopped moving entirely, inhaling his lust and exhaling her own. "Is that because you're dead set on protecting the business or yourself, Gabrielle?"

Both. She was so deeply invested in the Belleza that its best interests were gradually becoming her only interests. The Pearl was all she could claim, and though she tried to ignore the sadness in that, she couldn't deny that it was absorbing her life and she needed more than a restaurant could provide.

"There are too many risks to trading your account for my body. That's what we're really playing with now, aren't we? You give the Belleza a G&G Records's party and you get me in return. I don't make exchanges like that. As much as I want this account, I won't pay for it with sex."

"Good. Sex is sex. It's not business for me, either. I came to this resort because Cole acted like the food here opened up his world. I met a smartass waitress wearing Chuck Taylor high-tops who knew more about wine than most of the women I've hooked up with, and now I know she wants me as much as I want her. If that's not the clean business-personal distinction you want, then I'm sorry. It's what happened."

Gabrielle swallowed. She'd take this whole motion thing slowly, because if her body got ahead of her brain she was likely to end up straddled across his lap with her tongue in his mouth to stop him from saying so much stuff that made perfect sense. She wasn't about to feel ashamed of her choice to separate sex from business, yet she was on the fringes of wondering whether she put herself in a corner by denying herself to change her mind or make an exception for a man she was equally mindlessly and mindfully drawn to.

"I think you should go for an outdoor sunset party." Strictly business was the only approach she could take. Eventually he'd understand. And if not, he was free to turn his attraction to someone else. It wasn't as though there weren't legions of women aching for space in a record producer's bed.

Easing his intensity, Geoffrey listened to her suggestions and they stayed focused on what he wanted accomplished with this celebration and how the Belleza could enhance every moment.

"So. This gala's celebrating Phenom Jones. His music is R&B with heavy rock flavor. I *love* rock, by the way, and Phenom's sound's brilliantly unique. Anyway, I'd insist on the elbow room the outdoor options offer. It was listed in my notes from Robyn that he likes the outdoors, wide-open spaces. There's more room for instruments and dancing and especially dining. I think our goal should be to create an ambience and a menu that'll reflect him."

"You've never met Phenom," Geoffrey said.

"You have. You can convey what he wants."

"I'm not a messenger. This is a music industry event. Folks from other labels will be there. Get an insider's view of the industry, then."

"How would I do that?"

"Meet Phenom and some others who'll be at the party. Interact with them, observe them, and you'll get what you need to make this a success."

Success. That word was one of her weaknesses. She wanted to succeed in this business more than she'd ever admitted to anyone. If she had an obsession, it was her need to dodge failure…to prove to her estranged family that she didn't need their support for survival. She felt incomplete without it, but she was doing well to make it in California on her own merits.

"Tell me more about this meet and greet," she said.

"I'm holding a weekend recording session at my private studio upstate. You'd be my guest, but not bound to me. I won't force you. I don't get my thrills that way."

"What's in this for you, Geoffrey?"

"It'd be my chance to show you my life. As soon as we're done here you're going to put my name in Google and you'll read the gossip and look at pictures and think you know me based on some articles and interviews. But you'd be wrong. You don't like being wrong, so I'm going to give you the chance to be right about me."

"You can't decide whether my perception of you is wrong or right."

"No, I can't. You can. So which do you want to be?"

"This is the strangest invitation I've ever received. And this is including the sock hop in sixth grade. The guy asked me out in Klingon."

"You speak Klingon?"

"No. I was rushing to get to class before the bell and I just nodded to get him to quit talking to me and before I knew it, he was telling his friends that I said yes to going to the sock hop with him. It wasn't a horrible time." Relaxed, and warm under the heat of his gaze, Gabrielle took off her jacket and draped it over her lap. "Kind of fun, actually."

"My studio's part of a retreat that's on a hot springs. Think that'd be kind of fun for you, too?"

Gabrielle's eyes rounded. A hot springs? Wow!

Strictly business, Gabby. Strictly business. "I'm more concerned with it being a productive visit. I'll need to look at my calendar and discuss it with our event planner. And what about Roarke?"

There was no way in hell that the Pearl could spare both Gabrielle and Roarke for an entire weekend when their staffing problems had no firm solution. She had every confidence in her assistant's ability to manage her administrative duties in her absence, but she presented the question to gauge Geoffrey's intent. If he prohibited Roarke from joining them on this trip, then she wouldn't go. What she'd built for herself in California was her new life, and there was no room in it for possessive males. She was too in love with controlling herself to let someone else control her.

"I wouldn't expect you to take this trip without your assistant. So tell him he's invited, too."

Even though his answer pleased her, she couldn't smile. She couldn't be comforted. With Roarke at her side, she definitely wouldn't have any problems remaining professional at the music mogul's hot springs retreat. Without anyone from the resort watching over her, she'd fall victim to more moments like this—fantasizing less about work and more about working open Geoffrey's shirt buttons. "I should give you my direct contact information. And can I ask, since you're inviting me upstate to your retreat, does this mean the Belleza's a strong contender for your account?"

"It does. I wasn't sure yesterday, when I ordered my lunch and didn't get it, but you changed my opinion and you got my respect. Yeah, and the meal was damn amazing." He took the business card she held out to him. "Now that that's settled, I have a question for you. Why the red bra?"

Red bra? She glanced down at her chest. One of her newest acquisitions glared like a naughty carnal siren through her thin white top. She hadn't changed into one of her Gabby-customized Pearl uniforms and had forgotten that the reason she'd worn the red bra today was because it was perfectly hidden beneath her jacket. "I wore this for confidence. Some people drink double shot espressos for that extra zing and I've opted to wear fun lingerie. Uh, I was thinking it'd be business on top and party underneath."

"Why can't we be that way?"

"What way?"

"Business on top." His gaze unhurriedly dipped from her eyes to her mouth to her breasts. "Underneath a party. An intimate one, just you and me. Do you want that?"

"I want it," she finally said. "I *can't* want it, though. It'd be too complicated. The industry celebration's at the end of this month. If you choose the Belleza, I'll need to keep this a business relationship."

"After the celebration, then what? What if I said I'd wait for you to let this become something more?"

"Then I'd ask why, Geoffrey. Why wait for Gabrielle Royce when there are so many other women who'd be with you no matter what? Why wait for someone who puts business before anything else?"

"Gabrielle Royce is honest and complex, and I get the feeling men haven't been able to figure her out. I demand my chance to figure you out."

"Why, though?"

"A challenge like you is worth the wait."

She liked that he understood she was a challenge. She didn't simplify herself for any man, and he was the first who didn't call her a hassle and didn't turn away to spare himself the trouble of dealing with her. The men of her family's world had expected her to be a woman well groomed to bend to their will and never push back.

Geoffrey was beyond wealthy and famous, but he wasn't from the Royces' world. He had fortitude, strength that was almost overwhelming. He thought she was a worthy challenge.

"There's no guarantee between us, Geoffrey. I'm not promising you that after the party we're going to be together."

"Are you swearing that we won't be?"

"No. I can't predict what'd happen after the party."

"But you want to control what happens before then."

"Yeah. I'm not going to deny that. I like to be in direct control of my fate."

"I'm in direct control of mine. But think about this—now my fate is yours and yours is mine, so who's ruling us?"

"We both are." Gabrielle stood up and walked around the table to stand beside his chair. She wasn't a tease, wasn't trying to send mixed messages, but she was being drawn to him in a way that warned that perhaps neither of them were as in-control as they craved to be. "If you choose this resort, you can't have me. I won't have sex with you before the party. I won't cross that line."

"What if I said I'd be okay with that?" he said, standing up and bringing his body so close to hers. His soulful dark eyes made her want to admit things she had no good reason to feel when they contradicted what she'd been so certain about before yesterday. "What if I said I will wait for you? What if I told you that I want to make you mine?"

Don't believe him, her been-there-been-burned-by-that heart pleaded. How many men had used her to make alliances with her family or to build connections in her network of East Coast society somebodies? She'd never been anything more than a vehicle to men—something to joyride until something better came around the corner to appeal to their fickle tastes. No one had protected her from heartache, and she'd learned the cruel way to be her own defender. That wouldn't change now.

A career and incredible friends were all she had, and she wouldn't selfishly put them at risk. "If you said that to me, I'd ask you to look at your life and look at mine and realize that there'd be no point. All we could mean to each other is a casual hookup. So our choices are this. Just sex or just business. No overlap. Sex is great and all, but casual sex is fleeting. There's nothing behind it, so why sacrifice a business relationship?"

"Looking at the way you were dressed yesterday in the restaurant, I wouldn't have called you the practical type."

"You didn't know me yesterday and you barely know me now."

"If we work together, that's bound to change."

"I can handle that." *No, I can't. I'm lying. I can't handle battling myself and wanting you when I absolutely shouldn't.*

"When can I see your presentation?"

"My what?" Wasn't her fire-engine red bra presentation enough?

"The presentation. The 3D graphics?"

"Ohhhh!" Of course! She pulled on her jacket and checked her phone. This meeting had run past the time she'd allotted for it, but she still had time for an emergency girl-talk session before her shift. "Yes, let's meet up tomorrow evening, if that works for you. I won't have a kitchen shift and since I live in one of the staff condos here, I'm onsite most of the time."

"Tomorrow evening," he confirmed, so calmly that she wondered if she'd be mistaken to think he'd accepted her as out of his reach. A powerful man was not an invincible one. Geoffrey Girard might have the music world at his fingertips, but there were some things even he couldn't touch.

Gabrielle was one of them.

And that fact hurt her probably more than it hurt him.

"Where can you meet me?" Gabrielle, a decent distance away from the balcony and Geoffrey and the temptation to engage in naughty naked delights with the guy, gripped her phone against her ear.

She heard the catch of dread in Kimberly's voice. "What happened? Is there a problem at the Pearl?"

"No, no," Gabrielle interrupted. "And I'm grateful for that. Not another emergency, really. But I may have compromised an event and turned off a potential client. Where are you? Is Robyn with you?"

"Speak slowly, Gabby. When you panic, you start going a mile a second and then you act like you're about to combust. So before we get to that point, calm yourself down and get to the spa. Robyn should be here in a few. We have manicure appointments. How are your toes?"

Gabrielle's hands were so often submerged in water and food ingredients that she required biweekly paraffin dip treatments, but she never bothered with more than keeping her nails clean and healthy. Only for special events for which she wouldn't be prepping any food did she give in to manicures. But she overcompensated with pedicures. Her toenails were always stylishly decorated to perfection. "As much as I'd love a pedi today, I'm tight on time. But I'll be there in two shakes of a lamb's tail."

Laughing, Kimberly hung up. Gabrielle could count

on Kimberly's confidence and her inherited Parker powerfulness to ease a volatile situation. She still didn't know if she should tell Kimberly and Robyn that she and Geoffrey shared an attraction that could implode and take them all under. She didn't want to unnecessarily worry her friends, but as a professional it was her duty to inform them that she'd been terse with him yesterday and he hadn't yet agreed to host his industry event at the Belleza.

She went directly to the spa's VIP suite and knew she could talk without interruption. "Kim, where's Robs?"

Kimberly, perched on a plush swivel chair with her slim hands in the care of a nail tech, tossed her straight dark hair and said, "That was one shake of a lamb's tail. You're really wound up, aren't you?" She tipped her head toward the station next to her. "Sit here. Robyn's in the next room getting a margarita."

"I can't join y'all for nail treatments, but I *can* have a margarita." She raised her voice. "Hey, Robyn. Would you fix me whatever you're drinking?"

"Already took care of it." A moment later Robyn appeared with two glasses in hand. In a stunning summery dress and her long hair twisted into a bun, she looked more like a runway model than a behind-the-scenes event-planning genius. Handing a glass to Gabrielle, she sat on a vacant chair and sipped her margarita. "Kim said you were in hyper panic mode. Are you sure there's nothing going down at the Pearl?"

"Things are steady today. We still need someone to replace Shoshanna, but otherwise we're stable. This is about G&G Records."

"Geoffrey Girard, right?" Robyn asked, her hazel

eyes sparkling with intrigue. "I haven't met him face-to-face, but he has a voice that can melt ice. What's he like?"

Kimberly's nail tech glanced up as though to echo the question.

He's like every temptation that's bad for you, Gabrielle started to say. "He's intense. Really controlled. Not exactly angry, but…guarded. He reminds me of a pack leader, if that makes sense."

"*You* remind *me* of a pack leader," Robyn said, her brown skin glowing under a dusting of bronzer. "You're also controlled, guarded and intense. I guess the two of you are so similar that you didn't hit it off?"

Interesting. Was that part of the reason for her resistance? Did she see too much of herself in Geoffrey? "I met him yesterday, to be technical. He was dining at the Pearl and burst into the kitchen like he'd lost his damn mind. Wasn't it my duty to protect the kitchen?"

Groaning, Kimberly asked, "What did you do? Did you cuss him out, because I'm going to have to address that and get a jump on damage control."

"No, I didn't." She'd called him an asshole, but only in her mind. True, she'd all but straight-up admitted it on the balcony earlier, but technically it still didn't count as cussing him out. "Under the circumstances I was diplomatic and reasonable, but I just met with him and… I don't know if…um…"

"Good God, she's speechless," Robyn said, mystified. "Gabby, you're never speechless. Tell us what the deal is here."

"Suppose I'm not the person who should be working directly with him."

"That's crazy talk," Kimberly dismissed. "You're our executive chef."

She stole a few gulps of her margarita, buying herself an opportunity to regroup. She hadn't slept with Geoffrey—hadn't even tasted his lips. No action meant no harm and there really was no crisis. "Forget it. I'm sensitive to everything."

"Not that you don't have every right to be," Robyn muttered, setting aside her margarita and digging into her crocodile Fendi tote. "It's been a stressful couple of months, and to lose Shoshanna like that?"

"Speaking of Shoshanna," Gabrielle said, turning to Kimberly, "I visited her this morning and assured her that the sous-chef position would be waiting for her when she heals. I think she wants more security than my word. Is there something you and your parents can have drawn up for her?"

"Absolutely. I'm going to the hospital tonight, as a matter of fact. I'll take care of it."

"Thanks."

"People are calling her injury the result of a freak accident," Robyn said.

"I'm aware." Gabrielle sighed. "It's more hype to feed the 'haunted resort' rumors. Was it strange the way the wheel fell off the cart and how she was exactly at the wrong place at the wrong time? Hell, yes. But it's got nothing to do with the Belleza being haunted. Next we're going to have guests pulling out shovels and trying to dig up the grounds to find the supposed buried treasure."

"You're a nonbeliever?" Kimberly's technician asked, speaking for the first time since Gabrielle had come into the airy, ultramodern spa's VIP suite.

"I don't believe we're under attack by a pissed off spirit who's trying to protect some treasure that probably doesn't exist. The resort and spa has undergone numerous remodels, and has anything ever come up during any excavations in the history of this place? The answer's no. So when you ask me if I'm buying into this hype, the answer's no."

"And she's the free-spirited one among us," Robyn said. "To be honest, Gabby makes a lot of sense. This is a business and we need to be practical-minded for the sake of our guests and our company's publicity."

"I don't know what to think about all of this," Kimberly said quietly. "The fire last month, the reports of bad food—it's eerie."

"Malicious is what it is," Gabrielle insisted. "If someone's targeting us, it's not a spirit."

"What proof do we have of that?" Kimberly asked.

"None, but…" Shrugging, Gabrielle finished her margarita. "I can say that the Pearl can't afford to lose someone else the way we lost Shoshanna. Thankfully she'll recover from this, but it's going to be a slow and painful and frustrating recovery. I don't want to see another Belleza family member brought down like that."

"Who'd target the Ruby Retreat and the Pearl like this?" Robyn said to no one in particular. No one had the answer to that, but the question haunted them all the same.

"I sometimes feel that I'm not doing enough for the restaurant." Gabrielle set aside her glass. "I keep thinking the incident yesterday could've and should've been prevented."

"Gabby, you can't do this to yourself."

Someone had to. It was her kitchen, her team, her

responsibility. "I've been in this role for three years and just when I think I have it all under control, this all happens. None of this happened in Sean's tenure here."

Kimberly turned sharply at her older brother's name. They were estranged, with Sean responding to his sister's promotion by leaving the Parker family's company and starting up his own restaurant. Their younger brother, Ryan, was a musician and had no part of their tug-of-war. "Why'd you bring him up?"

"I took over his kitchen." Lazily she shrugged. "I should go to him, get some insight. Maybe we could have a meeting of minds…"

"Shut up. That's not funny."

Gabrielle rolled her eyes and twisted around to look at Robyn for backup, but the woman had frozen and looked at her as though she'd grown devil's horns. "All right, did we all agree to not speak *S-E-A-N*'s name around here or are both of you overreacting to a remark that doesn't mean anything?"

"You don't need Sean's coaching to run the Pearl," Robyn said carefully. "But…uh…have you been legitimately thinking about having a 'meeting of the minds' with him?"

"No, I was just saying something. Sean's been pretty careful about avoiding the Belleza since he and Kimberly fell out."

"It was his choice to hate on my promotion instead of supporting me," Kimberly defended. "Never forget that. Better yet, could you let him have his space and trust yourself to handle what's happening here? You don't need Sean's advice. All that would do is show him your weakness, which would only trigger him to assume that *I'm* a weak general manager. Leave him *and* Ryan alone, okay?"

"Fine." Gabrielle would've been more defensive had she not been appreciative. With her friends busy warning her away from the Parkers, they wouldn't be sharp enough to detect her pull toward Geoffrey. "I have something else to run by y'all. Geoffrey Girard has a recording studio in Northern Cali somewhere. He's invited me to some weekend get-together out there, where I'm supposed to meet Phenom Jones and a bunch of other industry folks, but the Pearl's already understaffed. I don't think I can be spared for an entire weekend, do you?"

"Go," Robyn said. "Get away from this for a couple of days."

"The studio's apparently on a hot springs. Talk about lap of luxury."

"In that case, *go!*"

"You're going," Kimberly decided, the snap in her eyes calmer now. "That's the perfect solution for you right now. Go to Girard's hot springs studio and when you come back maybe you won't be talking crazy anymore."

Robyn sat down again, with her iPad in hand. "The man is fine."

"What man?"

"Geoffrey Girard. God bless Google Images. Here's a picture of him at last year's Grammy Awards." She turned the tablet toward them and both Kimberly and her nail tech moaned a little.

What if I told you that I want to make you mine? Gabrielle stared at the tablet, recalling his words. Her heart felt as though it were spinning in her chest, and she wouldn't object to running into the next room to stuff some ice down her shirt. She envied her friends for being able to tease about him knowing that they weren't threatened by genuine attraction to him. If Gabrielle had given the man total control, she'd probably be naked with him now. She couldn't be with him out of the principle of the situation and because sex and business shouldn't mix—unless, naturally, sex *was* someone's business of choice.

"He's all right," she said, feigning indifference like the little liar she was.

"All right? Beautiful hair. I want to touch it. I love a nice fade on a brother." Robyn sighed, turning the tablet around so she could type. "On the phone he told me that Phenom Jones recently went platinum. The Belleza would be in a great position to have a share of that publicity." Her full lips formed an O. "Gabby. He has an eight-figure house in Beverly Hills and only lets a few people visit his retreat. A photographer interviewed him there once. It's located in a little unincorporated town called Storey Springs. Look at these photos. It's magnificent. If you don't go and report back the glories of that place, I'll consider it a personal insult and total disrespect to our ten-plus year friendship."

Gabrielle relented with a crooked smile. "I'm trying to not be offended that you two are so anxious to get rid of me for a couple of days."

"We're concerned for you," Kimberly clarified. Easing her hands from the tech, she came over to kneel in front of Gabrielle. "Gabby, look at me. We are concerned about the pressure beating you down. You've always been fierce, but these past several weeks have been hell on you, and Robyn and I aren't blind to it."

"What is this, some way to explain away why I wasn't gung ho about you getting with Jaxon Dunham? Stress wasn't to blame for that. It was how I honestly read the situation." Softening, Gabrielle pointed out, "But we're not friends because we agree on everything under the sun. You're in love now and I'm helping you plan your walk down the aisle, but I haven't changed my views of Belleza employees doling out sexual extras with guests. Every time I see Charlene Vincent flirt with some man in an expensive suit, I want to block her. By the way, she's gotten worse since you and Jaxon went public and I don't think that's a coincidence."

Gabrielle certainly couldn't indulge in an affair with Geoffrey when she was too fixed on the stance she'd taken against Kimberly and Jaxon. She refused to compromise her integrity, refused to be the hypocrite that stretched inside her every time she thought about Geoffrey.

"The repercussions of my relationship with Jax are real," Kimberly said, nodding as she returned to the tech, "but I can't be sorry for falling in love with the man I'm going to spend the rest of my life with."

"I don't want you to be sorry. I swear I want you to be happy. You too, Robs. I guess I just wish that romance wasn't so complicated. Even casual sex is complicated, and for no decent reason. I don't know how you two have managed steady relationships. I don't have what it takes to keep bouncing back when love knocks me on my ass."

"Crap. That's a mound of crap," Robyn decided. "You have a barrier around yourself, and as fearless as you are, the one thing that scares you is commitment. It's not about being hurt and rebounding. You're afraid to fall for someone."

"Whatever you say."

"I think you should go to Geoffrey Girard's studio and meet some folks. Get to know someone and see what happens."

"Robyn, for real, that's not an option. I'd be there to work, not fraternize."

"*You're* the one clinging to that distinction—that rule you won't bend. It's as if you want Kimberly and me to judge you and talk you out of this, but that's not about to happen. We want to see you happy, too. Even the kitchen staff is wondering how long you've been on the shelf."

Gabrielle remembered all too well from the discussion yesterday at the Pearl that her team was far too invested in her getting some action. "It's like everyone around me is pushing me, like a bird getting nudged out of the nest."

"Well," Robyn said, putting her tablet in her tote bag, "according to that bra you're wearing, I'd say you're ready to fly. Your jacket's open and that shirt's as good as transparent, little birdie."

Chapter 4

Gabrielle worked afternoon to closing, feeling like a liar every minute of her shift. At the spa she'd sat and watched her friends play-lust after Geoffrey and she'd shut down the legit feelings that were starting to brew. She'd convinced herself that she hadn't crossed lines with him, when the fact was, she had. Letting him kiss her finger? Line crossed. Confessing to him that she wanted him? Line crossed a gazillion times over.

Denying herself what he was primed to deliver seemed stupid now, as she confronted her empty condo later that night.

Gabrielle sat on her granite counter with a fat goblet of red wine and her laptop computer and sorted through the research she had compiled about the G&G Records party. In Dropbox and cloud severs, notebooks and emails she had everything she and her assistant had prepared for the meeting that had never really happened. As she opened a new window and abused the search engine, she told herself that researching Geoffrey's Storey Springs retreat was necessary for her to nab his account for the Belleza.

Situated practically a world away from the reliably sunny and sultry likes of Belleza and Beverly Hills, Storey Springs was at the northern tip of California and, yes, it possessed a hot spring. The spring, though, was privately owned by the same person who'd had a several-acre oasis constructed. It was Geoffrey Girard's property—all of it.

Gabrielle did a Google Images search and printed several photos, mostly scenery shots and those in the article Robyn had shown her earlier. As she gazed at the pictures, the realization settled. Next weekend she would be off to the secluded oasis, owned by a man who wanted to sleep with her. Excitement mingled with nervousness, and the more she repeated in her head that this had to be strictly a business trip, the more she didn't believe it.

The way her thoughts immediately slung to the electric-blue bra and panties set in her lingerie chest was proof.

In between manning the kitchen and running last-minute errands and giving instructions to her assistant, she had ducked home to change out of her pesto sauce–stained shirt and paused to admire the blue lingerie she'd bought in LA. It had beautiful lace and inspired all sorts of inappropriate wishes, but when she picked up the dainty material she'd started to imagine wearing it to Geoffrey's retreat.

Unofficially she'd decided she would go, and she'd

planned to wear electric-blue lace. Because unofficially she'd lost her mind.

Not yet done for the night, Gabrielle considered standing and stretching before she resumed her research, which had now drifted to scouring the results of a "Geoffrey Girard dating" inquiry. So far she knew he was a compulsive dater. By the time tabloids had him linked to one woman, he'd already moved on to another. And they were all tall with breasts that reminded her of Dolly Parton in *The Best Little Whorehouse in Texas*. Feeling strangely substandard, Gabrielle fit her hands over her breasts and considered them. She'd always considered them average—she couldn't get her own hands to cover them fully, but then again her hands had once been described as small.

Going to the fridge, she extracted a pint of Cherry Garcia flavored ice cream and was back on the counter with the computer on her lap and halfway through the pint when the bell rang.

Jerking as if she'd been caught doing something wrong, she swallowed down a lump of ice cream and watched her laptop coast down to the floor in a clatter that gutted her. Yelping an expletive, she hopped off the counter and growled, "Damn it, I'm coming!" to whomever had the audacity to touch that bell again.

"I can't be*lieve* this," she muttered, closing the laptop and putting it on the counter for later inspection after she got rid of the late-night visitor. It was probably one of her neighbor besties, and as much as she loved them, they weren't the high-tech geniuses she'd need to resurrect her computer. "That's what I get for multitasking when I should've just gone to bed."

When she opened the door, she leaned against the

jamb and looked expectantly at the six-foot-five chunk of sex appeal standing on the other side of her door. "What're you doing here?"

Yeah, good job acting as though a few minutes ago you weren't in your kitchen groping your breasts while cyber stalking him.

Geoffrey removed his hands from his jeans pockets and crossed his arms, making his muscles flex. "A bad time?"

"Midnight? Yeah, not the best time." She squeezed past him to look left and right. No Robyn or Kim out and about. Hopefully he hadn't drawn attention showing up here as conspicuously as he had. Was he *trying* to get her busted? "I didn't give you my addy."

Dude, how'd you find out where I live? she almost tacked on, but waited for what he'd say next.

"You told me you live at the resort. I ran into your assistant, Roarke, and he told me where I could find you if you weren't at the Pearl. Does that answer the question you were thinking about asking me?"

"Does it get boring, always having an answer at the ready?"

"Never." He hesitated, then asked, "Am I welcome inside your place?"

No, she should've said. *You're too irresistible and I'm too horny.*

"Yes, come in. Fewer questions to answer in the morning if my neighbors were to see you loitering outside my condo." Enjoying his uncertainty, she pulled him inside, shut the door and said, "The Pearl is closed for the night and I'm off the clock. You can't be expecting me to drop everything just because you rang my doorbell."

"You dropped something, based on the crash I heard in here and the mother-effer bomb that followed." He lifted a pair of solid, thick shoulders. "You weren't quiet about it."

"What, did it offend you? Not only are we both adults here, but I can cuss in the privacy of my own home."

"Actually, I like your dirty mouth."

Gabrielle had no good response to that. "Uh," she stammered. "Why are you here tonight? We said we'd meet again tomorrow. If there's a problem, the Belleza has an entire conflict resolution team to assist. Call CR. I can connect you now." She strode across the living room to pick up the cordless phone. When he didn't budge, she carried the phone to him.

"I don't have a complaint for CR. I'm here because you never gave me an answer about coming out to my studio."

"It's a lot to digest, Geoffrey. Abandon my duties for an entire two days at the peak of summer to spend a weekend with you? We didn't discuss the details. For one thing, what kind of drive are we talking?"

"We'd be taking my jet," he said in a murmur that made her stomach do a strange dance. "I want you to be there, Gabrielle. But is that what you want?"

The blue lace undies waiting in her bedroom cried yes. She shrugged. "It's an assignment. Part of my commitment to handling your event's needs with the utmost energy and care."

He paused. "You're right. Just an assignment."

Gabrielle tossed the phone from one hand to the other. "So are you going to get into specifics or are we going to pick this up tomorrow?"

"Hmm," he said, his eyes washing over her and stopping on her patriotic-themed toenail polish.

"What are you thinking?" she dared to ask.

"The same thing I thought when I first talked to you at the Pearl."

"You thought I was a waitress. An inept one."

"I thought you were so damn sexy."

A vivid flash of the day before surged through her head and she pressed her palms to her abdomen and suppressed a needy sigh. She was needy, all right. She needed something from this man. Not attention. Not even love. A touch. That's what she needed.

She did not need him to walk into her kitchen and point to her battered laptop and ask "Is this what hit the floor?"

"Yes," she said. "I may have killed it."

"I can take a look."

"Oh, you don't have to—"

But he did anyway. Geoffrey carefully opened the computer, and she was rushing over to grab it when he said, "Nice web of a crack on the screen. Upper left corner. Right off I'd say it's still breathing, but as a word of advice you might want to think about putting a password on it so your search isn't the first thing someone sees when they bring it out of sleep."

Gabrielle's feet were lead but she dragged herself to the counter where he stood and he turned the laptop toward her. There it was, her most recent search: "Geoffrey Girard girlfriend."

Mortified, she tried to gracefully slip out of this. "It's research. Those key words are common and…"

"Ask me."

"Huh?"

"Ask me if I have a girlfriend. Ask me whatever you're asking Google."

"Fine, then. Are you seeing someone?"

"No. That ended two months ago."

"Does she know it ended two months ago, or did you meet me and decide to kick some poor sucker to the curb?" Okay, that was harsh—brutal, even—but she'd witnessed it happen in her old world and knew that damaging relationships were just as common in La-La Land. "I want to know if you're breaking some woman's heart to get to me."

"I'm not a man who'd use a woman that way. You don't know me, so I wouldn't expect you to know that about me. But I'm in front of you and telling you and what I need to know is whether or not you trust me."

Conflicted, Gabrielle shook her head. "I can't do this. Why are we talking about trust anyway?"

"Because hopefully you'll be joining me at my vacation property and I want you to be comfortable."

"Let me ask you something, then. Are you inviting my competition to the studio, too?"

"There is no competition. It's only you. I've decided that the Belleza Resort and Spa will be the venue for Phenom's celebration."

The Belleza got the account! Recalling what Kimberly had said about the prospect of absorbing the publicity of the event, Gabrielle bounced up on her toes and flung her arms around Geoffrey.

One of his arms loosely held her against him, and she moaned before she could squelch. Undoing the trouble she was headed for, she quickly backed down. "I'm sorry."

"For what? Being excited that you secured an account?"

"For hugging you. I shouldn't have."

"I'm glad you did, Gabrielle."

"It's just business," she said. "Just an event."

"Is that what you want?"

"I already told you what I want. I can't have it. I can't have you." She'd be damned if she looked into his eyes while she said this. There was only so much disappointment she could handle, only so much she could demand of herself. "Anything else you care to know?"

"Yeah," he said in a whisper. "What's that gooey stuff on your chin?"

Gabrielle felt her cheeks flame and immediately scrubbed a hand over her face. "It's ice cream," she said.

"What flavor?"

"Cherry Garcia. Ben & Jerry's. Why are you so interested?"

He smiled a little and lifted a hand to brush aside a wayward strand of hair from her face. His thumb brushed her cheek ever-so-lightly. "So you and old boy Roarke are close, I take it?"

"What makes you ask?"

"The way he talked about you. Like you're the best thing to hit this earth since…since ice cream. And he's protective. He asked if I was between girlfriends when I told him we'd had our meeting on the balcony today. He thinks I'm out to make you my territory."

"Aren't you?"

"You're a woman, not territory. What happens between us is as much your choice as it is mine. I'm not interested in steering you to my bed tonight."

"But you'd happily steer me to *my* bed."

"Gotta admit, it's a shorter distance. And does it make me a bastard that I'm out-of-my-head-attracted to you?"

"No."

"I should also tell you that I got the impression that Roarke was trying to protect what's his."

Gabrielle searched his eyes, wondering what his angle was. She suspected jealousy, but why would he make up something like this about her assistant? "Roarke's my assistant and a nice guy. That's it."

"Mr. Nice Guy can't have a crush on his boss? You're not naive enough to believe that."

"It's late, Geoffrey."

"Yeah."

"I think, if I go to the studio next weekend, I'll drive. Alone."

"No Roarke coming along with you?"

"The Pearl can't spare us both."

He turned to go, but pivoted and touched her arm. "There's no point in you driving to Storey Springs. If you don't want to fly, I'll drive you."

She shook her head. "Nope." She hoped she wouldn't regret this. "I'll get on the jet, but if you'd like to ride to the airport with me, my only condition is that we take my car."

"What do you drive?"

"A Ford F350."

"Uh—"

"I swear, if you say that's a 'man's truck,' I'll slam my door in your face," she warned. Defeat washed over his face and he shrugged with his palms held up in all innocence.

"I was going to say that's a solid truck. Good space for somebody like me. I have height. Long legs."

"I noticed. Um, so then we're agreed?"

"Sure," he replied, and turned to leave.

Gabrielle snagged his sleeve. At his questioning glance, she hurriedly said, "If I'm going to pick you up, I'll need to know where to find you."

He wrote down the address. "We can talk more tomorrow."

"Definitely," she said, then escorted him out and returned to find her ice cream a liquid puddle in its container. After she disposed of it and jogged to her bathroom, she wondered if he'd shown up fully intending to catch her unguarded and depleted of good sense.

She'd been making bad choice after bad choice since she'd met the man, and wasn't likely to correct herself any time soon.

She drew a bubble bath, lit a couple of scented candles and sank into the tub.

She shivered, recalling how his eyes had swept over her. His attention had made her crazy wondering what he was thinking when his eyes dropped to her feet and then rose to her hips when she'd turned to grab the telephone. She'd pretended not to notice, but she *felt* his eyes on her.

Gabrielle let her head drop back as she stifled a yawn and shut her eyes against the candlelit atmosphere. The water felt so good caressing her skin…

So did Geoffrey's hands. So did his body.

Alone with him now, without the risk of being interrupted, in bed, not on a balcony, she wove her anxious fingers through his hair and felt him moan against the hollow of her throat. This was bad, deliciously bad for reasons she couldn't be bothered with now. All she was certain of was that she craved this chance to be bad, with him.

Geoffrey stilled to rake his eyes over her, satisfaction washing over his face at the sight of her, sweat-dampened and unkempt, her mouth parted and uttering desperate pleas for him to fill her. His palms cruised over her stomach until his fingers crept lower to make her whimper. He teased her, bringing her to the edge and then suddenly switching tempo.

He moved up her body again, pressing her deeper against the soft sheets, this time clasping her wrists in one hand and parting her thighs with the other. He demanded that she keep her gaze steady on his as he plunged inside her and emptied himself in her.

Then his head dropped and that amazing mouth drew in a taut nipple. His teeth scraped the sensitive flesh, causing her to arch against the wall of his whipcord-lean, nude body. His tongue soothed her until the first orgasm exploded through her.

Geoffrey alternated between her breasts until they were throbbing and sending shock waves straight to her clitoris. Then he slung one of her legs over his shoulder and licked her.

Again she broke, this time in his mouth as his tongue tortured her. She'd wanted to return the pleasure, to use her mouth on him, but he'd pressed her against the bed and rose above her. Finally he buried the hard length of himself into her and began to rock.

With each roll of his hips, she moaned into his mouth. He cupped a breast in his hand and gently squeezed and fondled while his tongue greedily sought and his hips grinded. Passion poured from her sobs as she writhed beneath him. Then his eyes, so dark and clouded with lust, locked on hers and she was every bit the hypocrite she never wanted to be.

On fire, Gabrielle jerked up and splashed water over the bathroom tile. Her heart pounded and she felt a deep throbbing sensation between her thighs. She clamped her legs together and slapped a hand over her flushed face.

Around her, the room had fallen dark because the candles had burned to puddles of wax. How long had she been asleep, dreaming of tireless banging? She climbed out of the cold water, toweled dry and padded naked to her bedroom. She'd spent half the night dreaming of steamy, reckless sex with a man who wanted to make her his next flavor of the week.

She slid into bed and pulled the covers up to her chin. No way could she keep living like this. It had been so long since she'd had sex that she'd forgotten what it felt like to move so intimately against someone else, to have his mouth discover and exploit every sexy crevice of her body...

She punched her pillow. At this rate, she'd never sleep peacefully. What she needed was a flat-out good lay, or some productive work to do.

Her only current reasonable option for sex was a stranger, someone far from Belleza, California. Even if Geoffrey was right about Roarke and the guy was cradling some crush on her, it didn't matter because he was dating someone else and he was her colleague. Sex with him would be the messiest complication she could bring down on herself.

Sex with Geoffrey Girard would be messy in the hot, delicious sense. He would move that perfect mouth downward, pausing to lick into her navel before continuing on to where he'd be holding her still with his strong, skillful hands bracing her quivering thighs open wide.

"Damn." Gabrielle kicked her covers aside, put on her most unattractive, *un*sexy pajamas and hurried downstairs to brew a pot of coffee and boot up her cracked laptop.

Chapter 5

Geoffrey was half expecting the ice-cold attitude the hostess served him when he showed up at the Pearl at seven for his meeting with Gabrielle. She'd suggested the time, saying her shift was over at five but she'd need some time to freshen up. Arriving on time, he stepped to the hostess's station to be escorted to a table.

Charlene stared him dead in the eye and walked away.

If looks could kill, he'd be six feet under.

"Can I help you out there?" a slow, gruff voice offered.

Turning around, Geoffrey saw an elderly man approaching. "You're that waiter from the other day. You took my order and disappeared. What the hell was that about?"

The man didn't deny the accusation. Instead, the old guy looked pretty damned pleased with himself. Nodding, he stuck out a gnarled hand. "Jonah Grady. I run the bar. The gatekeeper didn't seem all that friendly to you. Is there something I can do?"

Geoffrey glanced in the direction where Charlene had stormed off. "You weren't keen on helping me when I gave you that lunch order. I could wait for the hostess to come back and do her job."

"Charlene's eyes were shooting daggers at you," Jonah said. "I could see that from the bar. Care to step over for a drink? Advice is complimentary, you know."

"I'm meeting the executive chef," he said. "But all right, I'll take you up on that advice."

"No drink?" Jonah checked as he stepped behind the bar.

"No." Geoffrey didn't care if he was the only patron surrounding the bar who didn't have a drink front and center. A couple of days ago he'd considered refusing the sauvignon blanc that Gabrielle had served him, but he thought he had deserved the courtesy, all things considered. Now the waiter to blame was right here in his face, and he wanted the man to recognize what he'd done. "I wasn't all that okay with your level of service the other day. You needed to hear that from me, man to man."

Jonah took a cloth and began to fold it. "The Pearl made amends, I'm sure of it."

"I took my complaint directly to the head honcho— unintentionally. I thought she was a waitress at the time. She did make amends."

"Then pardon me if I don't feel regret for knocking over the first domino."

"What's that supposed to mean?"

"I saw Charlene give you her appraisal that day.

You may not have rejected her outright, but your body language did all the talking for you. And I thought I'd help you out by getting you the attention of a different sort of girl. That'd be Gabby."

"So you set me up so I'd get pissed off with management?"

"In a manner of speaking. Gabby is management here. As for you mistaking her for a waitress, that's not my doing. Now you're here again to see her." Jonah opened a bottle of FIJI Water and poured it over a glass of ice. "What I'd like to know, if you could humor a curious old man, is what you did to tick off Charlene."

Geoffrey accepted the water with a nod of thanks. "I made it clear that I'm not interested. Not in her."

Jonah chuckled. "You emphasized the *her*. I'd stake my tip bowl on which *her* has got your interest. It's not too hard to figure it out, if she's got you coming back here again and again." He sobered quickly then moved on to another patron, not before muttering, "And here she is. Try not to mess this up."

Geoffrey hadn't decided whether the bartender was out to help him or play games with his mind, and he was still undecided when Gabrielle appeared beside him in a tattered-hem Pearl T-shirt and tight black jeans. Her hair was pulled back from her face and secured with…

"Is that twine?" he asked, at the last minute stopping himself from reaching over to touch it.

"Twine? Oh!" Gabrielle's fingers fluttered over her hair. "Yeah. I snapped my elastic earlier and made do with what was handy. Listen, Geoffrey, we had a mishap with some spoiled fish today. No one has a decent explanation for this, but somehow the fridge storing our extremely hard to get high-quality Pacific fish became unplugged and you can imagine the loss. I'm sure you can now figure out why I'm still working and very late for our meeting."

She'd hesitated on the word *meeting*, looking around at the guests and bartender.

"I can wait."

"Geoffrey, I can't waste your time like this. I'm a mess and I probably still smell like fish." She made a face. "In fact, I should step back. I'm stepping back. Spoiled fish isn't the most attractive fragrance on a gal."

"You don't smell like fish." The look she fired at him had him laughing. "Nice side eye, Gabrielle, but I think you smell like steak."

She quit moving backward. "I just prepared a rib eye in red wine sauce for a guest. It's one of our classic dishes. Interested?"

Red wine sauce? "No, but I like the idea of you cooking for me. It makes me want to know if you'd let me do the same for you."

Gabrielle's cheeks, already borderline ruddy from the kitchen, flushed a deeper shade. "Quit."

"When can I get time with you?"

"I have about another half hour maybe, but I'll still be in my work clothes and generally unappealing. Not put-together and perfect like some."

Geoffrey followed her gaze to Charlene, who'd returned to her podium and was unabashedly watching them. "Gabrielle, the thing is, I'd rather be with you exactly as you are now than be with her. She's hot, yeah, but it's all on the surface. I don't know her, but I get the feeling she runs through men fast."

"As fast as you run through women?" Gabrielle crossed her arms. "Tabloids have you paired up with a list of good-looking, clearly artificially endowed ladies. I can't imagine how much money they must spend on special-made bras."

"Gabrielle, why are you finding reasons to push me away?"

"Because," she said quietly, "I can't keep myself away. Damn it, when I saw you here, I got so excited. And I shouldn't be excited to see you across a room. It's wrong."

"We agreed to meet up tonight. I'm not giving that up."

"I told you it'd be at least another thirty minutes."

"I heard you the first time."

"You'd wait that long for a woman who reeks of food, has twine in her hair and wears a B-cup?"

Geoffrey folded his hands over her shoulders and didn't give a damn who was watching. "I'm waiting for you. If you come back to me still smelling of food and with twine in your hair, I don't care."

Baffled, she jerked a nod then went through the kitchen's double doors. As he was turning back to the bar, Charlene caught his attention. She came over, frowned at the bartender and looped her arm around Geoffrey's.

"I'll get you a table."

"You weren't keen on doing that when I came here," he said.

"A table for two tonight?" Charlene asked, ignoring his comment. "I didn't see you come in with anyone. In fact, you seem very friendly with Gabby."

Keeping in mind Gabrielle's nervousness about anyone noticing their attraction and how determined he was to seduce her the way she ought to be seduced, he said neutrally, "She and I have business. A gala for one of my clients."

"You're hosting something here?" Charlene's glittering eyes widened and without asking permission, she sat in front of him. "When?"

"End of the month."

"Who's the client?"

"Phenom Jones."

"Oooohhhh!" Charlene squealed, and when folks around the room glanced at them, she laid her hand on his and smiled broadly. "Love him. Gabby hasn't brought me up to speed on your party, but I'm sure she will. We work closely together on functions like this. It's always a good idea to have a seasoned, polished hostess to greet your guests. I'll do my part to make sure the night is a success."

He began to move his hand, but she held him in a secure grip now.

"Oh, what stunning cuff links." She had both of his hands now and was rubbing her fingers over his wrists. "The music industry is rewarding, isn't it? I sing, you know. I had a YouTube channel but the Belleza asked me to close it because I violated some fine print in their employee agreement. But my friends and I hit up this club in Hollywood twice a month and sing karaoke. It's a regular thing and the club pays us now."

"I didn't know."

"If you'd called me, I would've told you."

"Charlene, I need you to take your hands off me." When she did without protest, he said, "What you want from me, you're not going to get. I get that it's tough

as hell to make it in California and in entertainment.
I swear to you, I get it. But I can't work with a woman
who thinks she can flirt her way to stardom. It takes
hard work and sometimes it's years before you see a
tangible payoff."

"All you'd have to do is give me a chance. I want to
have my own fame and my own money and…and control of myself. Give me a chance to have that. Come
to LA and listen to me sing. Or I'd sing for you right
now. If I sang for you now, would you let me record a
demo and put my name out there?"

"No, Charlene."

"See, you're only saying no because you haven't
heard me. I can do it right now, a cappella." Charlene
stood up and took authority, muscling his chair away
from the table with him still sitting in it. No band and
no backup, she leaped into a pop interpretation of Phenom's debut single, a gritty song about a man twisted
up in a string of lovers' deception. Her voice was light
but husky, and she brought the crowded dining room
to a halt when she belted out the chorus.

Geoffrey had to give her credit for the ballsy move
and he'd feel partly responsible for the hell she'd catch
for disrupting her place of employment for her own
personal gain.

When she finished, she asked through the echoing
roar of applause, "What do you think?"

"You're talented," he acknowledged.

"Geoffrey's right. You are talented." Gabrielle stood
beside Charlene. Her purse strap was slung over her
shoulder. "We're going to talk about this, tomorrow.
Right now there are some guests who'd appreciate

being seated. And next time, if you could not use the Pearl as your personal stage, that'd be awesome."

"Now will you call me?" Charlene asked Geoffrey.

"I said you're talented. I didn't say I could get you a deal."

Charlene huffed and marched away from his table.

"What in the name of... Okay, what was that all about? You're charming the jeans off me and the next thing I know you have the hostess standing in front of you singing in my restaurant."

"I didn't ask her to. I told her no, if you want the truth. You know what she did? She turned my chair around and sang anyway."

"That's Charlene, all right. She takes initiative. She's determined. And she goes about many things the absolute wrong way." Gabrielle watched him for a quiet moment. "Maybe someone like her is a better match for you."

"No, Gabrielle. Now you're wrong. She's like many women that I've been with, but I'm done with that cycle. I'm done being hunted by women who want me to be their route to fame and money." He got up and took her hand. "Come with me."

"Where?"

"The Ruby Retreat. I don't want to be here when Charlene gets the bright idea to come back for an encore."

Gabrielle wanted to feel more threatened by Charlene than she was. The hostess fit the profile of the women of Geoffrey's past, and clearly she was drawn to the man. She *did* have a fantastic singing voice, which had been a surprise to Gabrielle. She'd known the woman was trying to make a go of acting, but it seemed Geoffrey had inspired her to showcase a few other talents.

A throaty, attention-grabbing singing voice.

Hardcore flirting skill.

What she'd done, bursting into song for the dinner crowd, wasn't acceptable. But she'd taken the risk to get through to Geoffrey Girard.

Gabrielle was more familiar with that than she wanted to admit. She was courting all sorts of risks, but willing to do it because of him. He drove her to take chances and push boundaries further than she did on a daily basis. She'd always considered herself a free spirit, but now she seemed to be looking at herself and seeing someone caged and desperate for freedom.

She wanted to be free to pursue him and enjoy him.

She wanted what she just couldn't have. So she needed to resist whatever this was between them.

Entering the lounge, they were draped in red light and sultry music, and as she saw couples dancing and people crowding the bar, Gabrielle once again couldn't believe how beautifully the Ruby Retreat had recovered from last month's fire. That had been another crisis that was still oddly unexplained.

"Someone said this place was set on fire not too long ago," Geoffrey commented when they arrived at the bar and she ordered a cosmopolitan.

"I was just thinking about that," she said. "If you listen to local gossip, then you might be wondering if the Belleza's haunted after all. I don't think so, but I'm not getting much help controlling the rumors, what with our best bartender fanning the flames and filling people's heads with talk of treasure and spooky incidents."

"Would that be the old man on shift tonight?"

"He's the one. Jonah. A pain in the butt sometimes, but I love him."

"Naw, he didn't get into any of the treasure and haunted resort talk, but I've heard the rumors."

"And yet you chose the Belleza to host your gala. I appreciate your vote of confidence, Geoffrey." She smiled and held up her drink. "Are you going to order something?"

"Ginger ale."

"Oh, did Jonah fix you something stronger? The resort's kind of known for its incredible selection of liquor."

"No."

Gabrielle didn't press for an explanation but he offered one.

"I don't drink alcohol anymore. Not often."

"You don't?" She'd given him a bottle of blanc the other day, but had had no idea that he might be battling an addiction. "Are you an alcoholic?"

"Nah, but alcohol killed my family. My father was addicted. He could never seem to get a handle on it. My mama kicked him out of the house only to let him back in, over and over. It came to a point where he was drunk and had her and my brother in the car and he crashed it. I was in school when it happened. Got called to the principal's office to find out I had no family to go home to."

Gabrielle lost her taste for the cosmo. Putting down the glass, she said, "How awful. I had no clue."

"You didn't come across that on Google?"

She'd been too preoccupied with figuring out his dating status to realize he'd been so tragically orphaned. "Guess I wasn't looking for the right information. Who raised you?"

"Grandmother. Anyway, I don't want to get to the point where I start depending on a drink to get me through the night. I don't want to lose myself like that."

"You're already conscious of it and I think that gives you more control than maybe your father had."

"Why'd you put down your drink?"

"I don't want it anymore."

"Don't think you can't drink around me. I drink sometimes. Just not often and that's what I prefer. You don't have to change yourself to accommodate me."

"God, how is it that you know exactly what I need to hear before I've even realized that I need to hear it?"

"I'm just awesome like that."

Playfully, she cuffed his shoulder. "You're cocky."

Smoothly he clasped her hand and drew her closer. "If you're not going to finish that, then let's dance."

"I'm going to be the odd woman out on the dance floor. I'm still in my work clothes, remember?"

"You don't care about that. You like being different from everybody else. You wear cut-up shirts and Converse high-tops."

So he called her on her crap. Okay, she respected that. It'd do her body some good to loosen up on a dance floor, so why not?

Adjusting her cross-body purse, she let him guide her to the crush of gyrating bodies. The song was heavy on the bass and blended a man's rich, liquidy voice with piano and guitar.

Linking her hands around Geoffrey's neck felt as natural as swaying close until she was flush against him.

I shouldn't be doing this…

She gazed up at his lips and licked her own.

I shouldn't be letting him hold me like this...

He glided a hand down to her hip, curved it over her ass.

I shouldn't be wanting this...

Pressing tighter, following his lead, she moved with him. He had to be hypnotizing her—but then, she didn't believe in hypnosis or that anyone but she was responsible for her actions.

"I want you closer," he murmured onto her lips.

"I can tell." She raised her eyebrows and felt herself melt into a naughty smile. "How's this, then?"

Geoffrey's groan came from deep in his throat and she wanted to hear it again, so she circled her hips deliberately and got her reward.

"Would it be a problem if I paid to clear this room and get you alone?" he asked.

Alone? She couldn't give him that. Despite how suggestively they were dancing now, she was nervous about not being able to stop herself if they were alone and had no one around to remind her why going too far and wanting far too much would be terrible mistakes.

"What would you say to meeting me at the Pearl after closing?" she proposed. "I'll bring everything for the presentation I'd planned to show. It's mutual territory but will be private, too. You're still staying at the Belleza, right?"

He nodded. "I check out tomorrow."

"All right, well, how about meeting me tonight at eleven-thirty?"

"What about security?"

"Not to worry. I'll take care of it."

After that, they danced through another few songs

and Gabrielle reluctantly had to break away. The sooner she got back to her condo, the sooner she could get primped and polished to meet up with him again.

To discuss business. *Business.* She couldn't forget the core point in all of this. They were working together to make his record company's gala a sparkling success. Her horniness and his obvious arousal had zip to do with business.

Geoffrey insisted on driving her to the condo, where they agreed he'd swing by and pick her up at eleven thirty. That way, they could drive their respective rides at the end of their late-night meeting.

Gabrielle, who'd never ridden in a Bugatti before, was even more reluctant to leave behind the luxurious leather that seemed to contour her every curve. She especially didn't want to leave behind the cool, woodsy scent of the car's interior. It smelled like Geoffrey, and she wasn't going to lie to herself—she *really* liked his scent. Slipping out of the car, she was a bit guilty that she'd thought of him as an asshole that first day in the Pearl. He was more than a demanding guest or an intensely powerful male with a reputation as a Hollywood player. He'd been gutted before, was jaded and genuinely appreciated things that most men overlooked.

It didn't make her stupid or reckless to want to be around someone like him.

Did it?

Geoffrey walked her to the door, teasing, "I think I want a rib eye steak now."

"Ha. Ha. Ha. So funny. If you ever quit the music biz you should become a comedian," she retorted in her own sarcastic tease. Gabrielle had a fragrance in a crystal bottle on her vanity that'd make him forget all about steak.

Dipping forward, he gently held her waist. "Remember when I said there's a chance I'll kiss you again? This is that chance. What do you want to do with it?"

In the Ruby Retreat, she'd been locked, loaded and ready to rear up and kiss him hard and deep. She'd been so ready for his mouth, and she still was.

Her phone rang inside her handbag and she pulled it out to find Robyn's name on the caller ID. She sent a "can't talk now" message through and told him, "I'm going to take the ringing cell as a sign that I shouldn't go for that kiss. It's what I said earlier. I want you, but I can't want you. I'm sorry."

"Don't be sorry."

"Are you all right, though, Geoffrey?"

"Yeah. I'm not trying to make you feel threatened or forced. I'm just letting you know that when you're ready, I'll be ready."

"Or *if*. If I'm ready. It might not happen for us, even after the gala." She eased his hands from her waist. "See you at eleven-thirty."

"Eleven-thirty."

She waited until he was out of view before she unlocked her door and slipped inside the condo. She'd been close to putting her mouth on his, and then what kind of trouble would she be swimming in?

Two nights ago she'd decided to get herself to a club ASAP and hook up with a stranger, and now she was ransacking her closet for something sexy to wear for an after-hours rendezvous with Geoffrey Girard.

"I've lost my mind. Might as well have some fun before I find it," she declared when she opened her lingerie chest and plucked out the blue lace bra and panties set. She'd wear it underneath a sensible button-down shirt and the gray jeggings that had zippers up the sides. To accessorize, she'd pile on some necklaces and would go easy on the makeup.

Except she had plans for her lips. A lust-red shade would be the perfect pop of color.

She took her time showering and shampooing, then diffusing her hair. As eleven thirty approached, she had the strangest suspicion that something was about to happen. Whatever it was, it would change her. Only thing was, she didn't know whether the change would be one for the better or for worse.

On the border between sensible caution and inexplicable fear, she debated what she should do.

It wasn't too late to cancel. Or she could go forward and maybe keep her paws to herself. Men got a bad rap for their sexual appetite, she realized. She had sex on the brain and it was completely possible that she was insatiable.

A single bout of slap-and-tickle might not be enough. She might need more. She might need *him* more than she could've guessed.

"In that case, I'm screwed. I'm just not getting screwed." Rolling her eyes at the irony in that, she confronted a mirror.

Her cell rang and when she found Robyn's name on the display, she answered. "I totally meant to call you back earlier."

"Are you home?"

"Yes, but—"

"Good. I'll be over in five."

"But—" The phone beeped and she saw a call ended

message on the screen. Whoa, crap. With her long legs, Robyn would be striding over in two minutes tops, and then Gabrielle would have to come up with a reason to shoo her away at the door. She couldn't run the risk of her friend being here when Geoffrey arrived to take her to the Pearl.

Robyn would demand to know why they were meeting at the empty restaurant so late at night, just the two of them. She'd want to know why Gabrielle's assistant wasn't involved or she'd barge in on things, using her lead event planner trump card.

Rather than get tangled up in any of that, Gabrielle grabbed her tablet, the tiny pocketbook that fit her phone, ID and a credit card, and scooted out of the condo just as Robyn was approaching.

"Hey, where's the fire?" Robyn said, practically skidding to a halt.

"Oh, don't say that! After what happened at the Ruby, I'm more concerned than ever about not living in a single-family home."

"Sorry. But really, why are you running out of your place? I just told you I was coming over. I thought we'd eat sweets and look at some bridesmaid dress designs online."

"Yeah, I was going to tell you that I actually am on my way out." Gabrielle felt like an ass when she saw Robyn's expression dim. "Sorry," she parroted.

"It's cool. Um, you look really good, girl. Are these date clothes?"

"These? No, not these. I'm not going on a date." *Liar. I'm a liar. I am going on a date. A pseudo-date.* "I'm taking some time, going off on my own for a while."

"Yeah, you do that every so often," Robyn said. That was true. Gabrielle, Kim and Robyn worked together, practically lived together and hung out together. Though these days Kim was sharing more of herself with Jaxon, they were all still close-knit and Gabrielle had always found comfort in getting away occasionally. She took long drives to nowhere, found walking trails and, her favorite, searched for old California buildings to tour. "Please be safe. I could never go off alone like that. You worry me when you take off on those dangerous adventures of yours."

"Stop worrying," she said, taking Robyn's elbow and steering her back to her condo. "I always play it safe."

Too safe.

In case Robyn got wise to things and decided to pop out of her condo again to see what Gabrielle was really up to, she opted to wait for Geoffrey in the lobby.

"I feel like I'm sneaking around," she said when she got into his car. "If one of my friends catches us…"

"Gabrielle, why wouldn't your friends support you spending some time with a man who wants to be with you? Is your job really going to be on the line if you and I got more personal?"

"It's not about following the rules of some company handbook. It's an unwritten rule, really, about staff getting cozy with guests. I am in agreement of that unwritten rule. I have to stand by that."

Geoffrey didn't say anything until they were outside of the Pearl. "So that's it? You can't change your opinion?"

"I don't want to turn myself into a hypocrite."

"A hypocrite? What—"

"Never mind. Let's go in and talk about the gala."

Passing the night security, Gabrielle led him into the restaurant. The quiet and darkness didn't scare her—she'd spent many nights holed up here experimenting with recipes or finishing paperwork. Not much frightened her, but the idea that she could lose control of herself with Geoffrey had her shaking.

"You find your way easy in the dark," he said behind her.

"I know this place much too well. It's home."

Turning on a few lights throughout the dining room, she went into the kitchen and ended up inviting him in. Sitting on stools at one of the stainless steel counters, they viewed a presentation on her tablet and discussed themes for the gala. Agreeing to an outdoor space around one of the Belleza's luxurious pools that would afford the guests priceless views of mountains, they discussed menu options and were leaning toward a coastal feel when Gabrielle said, "I'm hungry now."

"It's one. We've been talking for over an hour."

"And we've accomplished so much." She held up her hand for a high-five. "Win!"

"I can't think of a better place to be sitting when I realize I need food." Geoffrey got off his stool and turned around. "This is the largest kitchen I've ever seen."

"It doesn't seem large at all when we're fully staffed and everyone's doing a task. We push and yell and complain, but generally we all like each other and get over the cramped kitchen." She put down her tablet. "Geoffrey, remember that chocolate sauce we were thinking about for the gala? What if you made it right now?"

"I don't know how," he responded slowly.

"You will. I'm going to show you." She patted his chest. "Aren't you glad you didn't go with another restaurant? I'll not only provide top-notch food, but I'm throwing in a cooking lesson. Roll up your sleeves and wash up at the scrub sink over there."

When his hands were nice and soapy, she wiggled in to wash her own.

"You've been preparing food for most of the day and you're going to give me a cooking lesson? That's passion."

"I love being a chef. Every day it's almost surreal that this is my kitchen, that this world is mine."

"So cooking professionally was something you fought for," he said, rinsing and reaching for a paper towel.

"That's exactly right." The Royces hadn't funded culinary school, but had instead shipped her off first to Harvard and then to Europe, hoping she'd come back to the States with her mind right and would attend graduate school to become either a doctor or a lawyer, as her brothers had. She'd resisted what her parents had wanted for her. That part of her life was the polar opposite of what she'd built here, so she kept her family out of the conversation. "Cutting into this industry wasn't easy for me."

"How'd you get your start?"

"Actually, my grandmother funded my culinary education. I couldn't afford Le Cordon Bleu or any of my research. She gave me the money and it was up to me to make the most of it." She smiled a little, thinking of her grandmother May. "I like to think I succeeded in that."

"I'd say you did. My success wasn't handed to me, either."

"You're as driven as I am."

He nodded solemnly. "What else wasn't easy, aside from the money factor?"

"There's a lot of insincerity in culinary arts. Reminds me of the fashion world in many respects." She dried her hands and started to pull the ingredients and utensils for the chocolate sauce. "Hey, what if we did something more with this? What about making it a peppermint sauce?"

"You're the boss."

"Oh, wow. You're genuinely relinquishing control?"

"I'm not an idiot. This kitchen is your turf. I'm an interloper."

"You are not. You're a guest. And you've been delightful." She paused with a saucepan in her hands. "I'm kind of having fun."

"Spending the night in a kitchen figuring out menus and cooking chocolate sauce is a hell of a cry away from what I might be doing if I hadn't met you. I'd be in somebody's VIP lounge, surrounded by people who grin in my face while they're holding the knife they want to put in my back."

"That vicious, huh?"

"I *wish* the music industry was just 'insincere.'"

She set up a prep station and set the pan on a burner. "So in the middle of backstabbers and gold-diggers are the rare gems who turn out to be great people to work with and who make you money. In the middle of the old boys' network in the New York culinary world were chefs out to crush my spirit and cooking school students willing to sabotage one another for celebrity status. Could be because of my youth or my sex or the color of my skin, but I was very often shut out of opportunities. Before I began working for the resort, I was treated like a neophyte. But buried underneath all of that was food. The food is my reason for fighting through the hell." Going to the prep station, she checked the ingredients. "Cooking has so many facets, but above everything I love the way a meal or even the aroma of one can elicit a memory."

"What memory are you going to take away from peppermint sauce?" he asked. He didn't look at her and she was glad, because her expression might betray her.

"Being with you."

Well, she didn't need her expression to give her away. Her voice did the honors.

"So to get started," she rushed to say, "we want to achieve a sauce that has a silky texture. Now it's time for you to make a decision. Peppermint extract is common, but some people experiment with vanilla. What's your gut telling you?"

"That I'm hungry now, too."

"Geoffrey," she said on an exasperated sigh.

"Sorry. I am hungry, though. It's all these ingredients and all the pictures we browsed online. I eat first with my eyes, then my nose, then my mouth gets in on the action."

Kiss him. Right now.

She throttled the thought. Just because what he'd just said was exactly what she'd once told someone in cooking school years ago wasn't cause to jump on him as if he was the last guy on earth. They were the only man and the only woman in the universe that was this kitchen.

"This won't take long," she promised. "If you follow my directions and this turns out perfect, I'll feed you. So what's it going to be? Peppermint extract or vanilla?"

"Make it peppermint. I'm going to want to pour this on some vanilla ice cream and don't want overkill."

"Okay, that's sensible. Next lesson, we're going to take some risks. You're a big boy. You can handle it."

As she guided him to stir in cocoa and salt, sugar and cream, they chatted at random and it felt as natural as it had to simulate dry-humping with him on the dance floor in the Ruby Retreat earlier tonight. Why was it so easy to be wrong? Why did it feel so exhilarating to be bad?

Somewhere in the process, she took the spoon and managed the constant stirring of the sauce. But he remained close, and the heat from his body rivaled the heat rising from the range.

"I want a taste, Gabby. Just one."

"Better beware. It might be hotter than you can handle." Giving the peppermint chocolate sauce another graceful stir, Gabrielle set the spoon on the ceramic cradle and faced Geoffrey.

Maybe she should've stayed where she was, confronting heat and flame. Then she wouldn't have witnessed dark need drop over his expression, as though he accepted her warning as an invitation.

As long as she was on the "should've" train, she should've reconsidered this private baking lesson. Or at least considered why she'd changed out of her girl's-best-friend T-shirt bra and boyfriend-style undies and into electric-blue lace before meeting him tonight.

Outside the sky was filled with secrets and silent, winking stars, and here in California's most provocative kitchen was nothing to counteract her lust-spiced attraction to a man as bad for her as the decadence simmering in the saucepan. Nothing except a chocolate-smothered spoon.

"Well," he said, as she picked up the spoon and held it out to ward him off while she tried to remember all the reasons why it'd be wrong to unbutton his expensive shirt and trace that buffet of muscle and almond-colored skin with her tongue, "I'm thinking there're a couple of ways to find out."

Gabrielle whirled to stir the sauce again. Work was the best distraction. Work was safe. Work was all she needed. "It's not ready to be tasted, Geoffrey."

"It is," he said quietly. "All the ingredients are there. So first, a taste. Then I'm going to appreciate it and enjoy it."

With a simmering saucepan in front of her, and Geoffrey Girard behind her, she was surrounded by heat. Taking the spoon, she escaped to the island. Somewhere under the array of pans and baking sheets was a countertop. "I wasn't talking about the chocolate."

Geoffrey cut the space between them, giving the spoon a single lick before taking it from her. Gabrielle hardly registered the noise of bakeware striking the floor, because desire drowned her every sense as he seized her hips, hefted her onto the stainless steel and licked into her needy mouth. "Neither was I."

She was more ready for him than she would've ever believed. Her tongue lapped at the sauce on his, her short fingernails dug into his shoulders. She wanted to claw through the expensive fabric to touch his bare skin.

This was their universe, wasn't it? So if she wanted to touch him, it was her right.

"Damn," he moaned. "Those red lips. Those beautiful red lips. I've been wanting to kiss you every other minute since I saw your mouth tonight."

"You're messing up my lipstick."

"I don't care." He roughly began to peel open her shirt, revealing the lace bra. "Do you?"

"Uh-uh. Actually, I care more about the fact that I have a need to get my hands on your body and you still have your clothes on. It's kind of a problem for me. So could you—"

"Chef Royce? Is there a problem— *Whoa!*"

Gabrielle squeaked and shoved at Geoffrey, but the night watchman who'd greeted her at the door had already come into the kitchen to get a clear, unmistakable view of her sitting half-naked on a counter with a music mogul between her legs.

"Shit!" she blurted, then covered her mouth with both hands when it would've done her more good to close her shirt. "He caught us doing it."

"We didn't get *that* far," Geoffrey said wryly, letting her hop off the counter.

"I heard the crash," the guard said. His face was calm except for the deep ruddiness coloring his cheeks. "Uh, the Parkers doubled up on security after the fire and everybody's extra cautious with the stuff that's been happening."

"We knocked over some pans," she said lamely. "I'm sorry."

"Whatever you're boiling here? It doesn't look too good."

The sauce! What had gotten into her? She knew what had been *about* to get into her, but as Geoffrey had said, they didn't get that far.

"Anybody been stirring this?" the guard asked, turning off the burner. "Not to tell you how to do your job, Chef Royce, but when it comes to sauce, you gotta keep stirring."

"I'm aware of that." *I got distracted trying to screw Geoffrey Girard while also baking peppermint chocolate sauce. Multitasking isn't for the weak.*

"Uh," the guard said, "your shirt."

She pinched the front together while grabbing a clean spoon and taking it to the range. "Thank you, but I've got things under control now."

"You sure?" His narrow-eyed glance landed on Geoffrey, then back.

"I'm sure." She wouldn't lose herself with Geoffrey. It was more dangerous than she'd expected. She'd left sauce burning in a pan and had gotten caught with her hands full of his shirt. She'd *better* have things under control. "There was no incident here, so if you could give me your discretion, I'd be grateful."

Again he looked at the two of them, then he sighed. "All right. No incident, nothing to report to nobody."

"Thank you." When he left, she studied the contents of the saucepan then faced Geoffrey. "This didn't turn out the way I thought it would. I don't think we should do this again."

"You didn't become a master chef by giving up after the first try."

"Not the chocolate sauce. I'm talking about the night." It was cowardly of her, but she avoided his eyes. "I'll clean this up. You should go. Since you're checking out tomorrow—oh, technically today—we should communicate by phone and email and you can get a hold of my assistant to schedule the next appointment. We should also be keeping our lead event planner in the loop."

"Back to strictly business, Gabrielle?"

"I've never burned sauce and gotten caught with my bra out when I was strictly business with a client, so yes. Strictly business." She waited until she heard the doors open with a swish and his footsteps fade before she said, "Good night, Geoffrey."

Chapter 6

Geoffrey had messed up. He'd fallen for a woman desperate to resist what they mutually wanted and now he couldn't even move on. Only hours after leaving Gabrielle at the Pearl, he leaned against the doorjamb of his rental cottage at the Belleza and watched his neighbor sashay away, taking her smooth long legs and kinky proposition with her.

At five o'clock this morning she'd begun mixing cocktails on her balcony. He knew that because dreams starring a very unattainable woman had forced him out of bed and to his living area to work out his frustrations on his dumbbells and bench press. The resort had a state-of-the-art gym, but he wasn't in the mood for conversation. At some point his neighbor had noticed the lights on in his cottage and made a trip across the courtyard clad in nothing more than a red silk bathrobe and a sly grin on her deep brown face.

And he'd declined her offer. *Stupid.* The twinkle in her eyes and the way she trailed a pink lacquered nail down his sweat-dampened chest told him she was fully capable of giving him a better workout than his weight bench.

But when he looked at her his raw male instincts suddenly shut off. Dora Truman was all wrong for the part. She was a few inches too tall, her hair the wrong color and her voice far too eager. Since the day he checked in and accidentally caught full view of her sunbathing stark naked on her balcony, he'd been curious about the woman other neighbors referred to as erratic and a charity case with more money than brains. As simple as it would've been to take her up on her offer, having her on a silver platter didn't stir a reaction.

Dora wasn't the woman he'd dreamed about introducing to completely untamed, and in some states illegal, sex.

That woman was cautiously making her way to his door. As the two women passed each other, Gabrielle paused to respond to something Dora said. Her soft laughter sounded strained and polite and wrapped around Geoffrey.

"Morning." When she didn't answer right off, he nudged the door open wider and offered, "Why don't you come in and have a cup of coffee while I hop in the shower for a sec?"

"I can say my piece quickly and leave." She plastered an incredibly fake smile to her face. "Obviously, I'm interrupting something." Her gaze wandered to the uncovered picture windows in his living room and landed on Dora, who had now returned to her cocktails. "She looks like she's not planning to drink alone. Were you going to go over there and join her?"

"I told you I don't drink often. Especially not at sunrise when I have a drive to Beverly Hills ahead of me."

Yanking himself from a memory of Gabrielle in his arms at the Pearl, he forced a cough to clear his throat. He looked at her to read her thoughts but ended up focusing on the enticing way her slinky white top clung to her torso and how her designer jeans hugged her hips just right. It would be so easy to forget his purpose and just kiss her. One little taste was all he needed to soothe the boil of his blood.

Gabrielle met his gaze dead-on. "She's pretty. Extravagant. An extrovert. She's your type, you know."

"You said that about Charlene."

"Your neighbor fits the profile, too. Your type is uncomplicated. Easygoing. Decisive when it comes to finding a man they want and going after him. I'm not like that." A slight frown had worked its way to her lush mouth, and her shoulders, bared by the skimpy cut of her top, were rigid with tension.

Could it be…? Geoffrey's eyes flickered behind Gabrielle to Dora's front porch and his ego purred like a kitten. She was jealous. "Dora's friendly."

"That she is," she said. She shifted her oversized tote bag against her side and cast a leisurely look from his head down.

Immediately, he became fully conscious that he was standing a few feet from her shirtless, rumpled and sweaty. "I was going to shower but Dora came over and now you."

"Uh, I'm intruding. I just got the idea to come here and talk to you, but this is a bad time. Your basic hygiene overrules my need to babble an apology for what happened at the restaurant."

"You were going to apologize to me?"

"Yeah."

"Then don't leave. Be back in five," he said.

"No, ten. You need to shave. You look dangerous. You look like a threat to my virtue."

"I'm getting damn good at deciphering your sarcasm."

"Good for you."

He ignored the clipped edge in her tone. He didn't want to provoke an argument. It would only make extracting that apology from her more difficult. And he could do without more difficulties. "Go ahead and have a seat. Remote's on the coffee table and there's coffee in the kitchen."

Her shoes clicked against the hardwood floor as she headed to the door. "Thanks, but no. I'll wait in my truck until you're ready to hear what I came here to say."

"No problem here. Shut the door behind you." With that, he strode off down the short hallway and went into the bathroom.

Gabrielle had gone from in control to out of control in sixty flat. She hurried down the front walk of the cottage, sucking in what was supposed to be a deep cleansing breath but ended up filling her lungs with the scent of saltwater, charcoal and grilled meat—a weird combo for such an early hour. She glanced over her shoulder at Geoffrey's rental cottage.

She'd come *so* close to launching at him and demanding that he take her. That would've been a horrible choice, being that probably no less than a half hour ago that Dora woman was wrapped around him like a ribbon.

It crushed her balloon of hope that he was still interested in her, but at the same time it sort of relieved her. The thought of him sleeping with someone else kept her focused on what her objective was: to make his company's gala a perfect event and promote the Belleza without letting anyone or anything get in her way.

If only she could brush off the part of her that went certifiable whenever he was near. The way his eyes flickered, how his muscles bunched when he crossed his arms, and the sexy half smile his mouth curved into when he was being a cocky jerk completely turned her on.

Apparently, it also turned on Neighbor Dora.

Gabrielle leaned her backside against the side of her car, grabbed her cell phone and dialed her assistant's number, trying hard not to compare herself to Geoffrey's Barbie-esque neighbor. When an automated voice mail greeted her, she put the phone in her bag and compared away. Dora was super tall and Gabrielle was not. Dora probably wore an E-cup, and Gabrielle filled a 32B. Dora was obviously a woman who went after whatever and whomever she wanted.

Gabrielle went after *whatever* she wanted, but the *whomever* was another matter.

"Hi there," called Dora from her patio. She waved a martini glass. "He's making you wait, is he?" Not giving Gabrielle the chance to answer, she snorted dry laughter. "Don't feel too bad, gorgeous. He's been making me wait since the day he moved in. It's starting to get boring, to tell you the truth."

Gabrielle wrinkled her nose in confusion. "What does that mean?"

"He doesn't take the bait too easily." Dora sipped her drink and perched on a patio chair, and her short robe slid too far up her thighs. In her tipsy haze, she squinted across the courtyard. "It must be the sweet ones he likes. Hmm, tell you what. Come over here and have a cocktail with me."

Gabrielle almost asked if the woman was planning to sleep with him. But she'd rejected him over and over and though she was here to apologize for being abrupt at the restaurant when the guard had walked in on them, she realized there were only so many times she could push someone away before he accepted defeat. His dalliance with this woman was his concern, and not Gabrielle's. She wasn't at risk of becoming a side fling, because they weren't going to kiss again. "Some other time," she called to Dora.

The woman huffed dramatically. "You sound like him. I suppose the two of you think three's a crowd?"

Huh? "Did he tell you we're dating or something?"

"Aren't you? I can't understand why he'd turned me down, unless there was somebody else."

Gabrielle left the woman alone with her wondering and registered that Geoffrey hadn't been mattress dancing with his cottage neighbor after all. Jealousy had worked her up for nothing. Now that she considered it, there *had* been dumbbells on the floor near a weight bench.

Guilt slithered around her. He'd been working out, not working Neighbor Dora. No doubt he'd noticed that she'd acted like she sat on a cactus. That apology she was planning on delivering? She'd need to make it a double. Trust was more sacred than anything, and she hadn't given him a chance to earn hers. Her personal drama aside, she owed him respect.

Avoiding Dora's intrigued stare, she turned and headed for the cottage. Glad that Geoffrey hadn't locked the door, she reentered the cottage and found two suitcases stacked on the sofa in the living room. It reminded her that in only a handful of days she'd be joining him in Storey Springs, and this time they'd be on his turf. If the invitation was still open.

She'd move aside the luggage and sit down as he'd offered, and when he got out the shower they'd maybe have a cup of coffee together and the tension between them would soften.

She grabbed the suitcases' handles and was startled to find one of them to be heavier than the other. Shifting to manage with the uneven weight, she grunted and hauled them up at her sides. As she turned, her eyes darted to a flash of movement to her left.

Geoffrey had moved swiftly, but not quick enough to spare her a glimpse of the dark patch of hair just below his abdomen.

"Damn it, Gabrielle!" he growled as his hand shot out to drag a throw blanket off a chair to wrap around his waist. He swore and hastily knotted the towel. "What the hell are you doing in here? You said you'd wait outside."

Her hands full, Gabrielle squeezed her eyes shut. "Don't you dare insinuate that I actually planned this. I'm not a peeper."

"Answer my question," he demanded.

"Fine," she replied curtly. "I figured I'd move your suitcases off the couch so I could sit down and we'd talk over coffee like normal people do. I should've called out that I was here, but other than that, don't put the blame on me."

"Open your eyes."

"I didn't see anything," she said automatically. It was partially true. All she saw was the distinct arrow of hair trailing down his stomach to the curly mass between his thighs. "Really, you moved fast enough to spare us both that embarrassment."

"You didn't see anything?" His enigmatic dark eyes considered her as he slinked toward her. He forcefully snatched the heavier of the two suitcases. "Why is it that I don't believe you?"

"Maybe you just have an overly suspicious mind," she returned, annoyed. "Did you think I came up here to rifle through your things, see if you packed boxers or briefs?"

Geoffrey dragged his free hand through his wet hair but he said nothing.

"I saw pubes. There, now that's the full truth."

Still, he said nothing.

"I don't need this," she said finally, setting the suitcase down. "If you want to go back and forth with me, you should know that it's not productive for either of us. If you still intend to include me in your weekend get-together, we could chat about that. Or you can simply forget that I was here in the first place."

Suddenly, he was only an inch away. She saw a muscle in his jaw twitch. "There are other things I'd rather do with you...to you."

She shivered. Her head felt lighter than a speck of dust. A fraction of a moment passed before she was pressed against him. She clutched his shoulders and hoisted herself up tight to the hard wall of his body. She tipped her face up and sniffed his aftershave lotion, and then she tasted the sensitive skin on the underside of his jaw. "Touch me," she commanded, nipping him. *"Now."*

A groan escaping, he molded his hands to her bottom and sank his teeth into her bare shoulder. "Is this what you want?"

Not really, it wasn't. She wanted to be intimate with a man she trusted fully. She wanted to be with him, just like in the dreams that had stolen her sleep. But her sensors warned her that Geoffrey might not be dangerous, but *she* was dangerous when she was with him.

He released her. "It wasn't a rhetorical question, Gabrielle."

She silently watched him disappear down the hall and tried to clear away the cobwebs of confusion. Were men always such work? Maybe she'd been out of the dating scene longer than she'd thought. Or maybe she was simply expecting more from him than he could give.

Clearly, he had issues of his own. The biggest was most likely his quest to avoid serious relationships. But even that couldn't explain his conflict of being aloof toward her one minute and then hot for her the next.

Unless this was all part of some off-the-wall scheme to toy with her...

A good girl wouldn't fight fire with fire. She wasn't a good girl anymore. Somewhere between finishing boarding school at Merriweather and bursting into culinary arts, she'd lost her halo and wasn't interested in recovering it.

Geoffrey returned dressed in jeans and a chambray

shirt. "Okay, let's go. I've got to pack up my car and check out, so we can talk while I get that done." He grabbed both suitcases and followed her outside. As he locked the door, she grabbed one of the suitcases and started down the walk.

"Your neighbor and I had a nice little chat while you were lathering up," she said loftily. She angled her head and watched his brows furrow.

"So that must be why the jealousy disappeared."

"Jealousy?" she echoed, and waited for him to pop open the Bugatti's trunk so they could store his luggage.

With the sun rising at his back, he looked gorgeous and all too sure of himself. "You heard me. You saw her leave my place dressed in nearly nothing and it got your back up. No need to deny it."

"Arrogant ass."

He had the nerve to chuckle as he shut the trunk. "Are you no longer planning on apologizing to me?"

"No, I am. I'm sorry if I seemed as if I was blaming you for the guard coming in and finding us…well, like that. We both got carried away too fast and the truth is, I bear the responsibility."

"You didn't force me to kiss you. I'm not your victim."

"And I'm not yours. I'm just clearing the air here. We can agree that we're both at fault and it's now understood that it can't happen again."

"If that's what you want."

"Stop throwing that at me. You already know damn well what I want, and why I can't go for it. What I want doesn't matter in this. What's best for the resort and your company's party—that's what matters. Can we be clear on that?"

"Okay." But from his grim expression, it didn't look as if it was.

"About Storey Springs. Do you still want me there?"

"You weren't invited on the condition that we sleep together. So yeah, I still want you there. I want you to meet my people."

"Then I will." Frustrated that her body still demanded his, she got in her truck and turned the key in the ignition with more force than necessary and rocketed onto the main road. He was going back to the Hills today, but that changed nothing between them.

The attraction was still raising hell, and they were both too deep in it to get out.

"It's not the same without you."

From her hospital bed, with her broken leg in traction, Shoshanna craned her neck to look toward the door and she winced. "*Govno!* I'm not used to the burns and this horrible cast yet. I feel like I haven't cooked anything in years." She crooked her fingers. "Come in, Gabby. Tell me lots more about how you're all suffering without me. I have to know someone's as miserable as I am."

Gabrielle entered the small room and took the visitor's chair. "We're all completely at loose ends without our resident sexy Russian chef."

"That's overdoing it." Shoshanna smirked.

"Completely serious. No one's cracked a potty humor joke in days *and* we're all lost without your hookup reports. The men of Belleza are suffering from a sex crisis with you laid up like this."

Shoshanna grunted a laugh. "You make me sound like a ho."

"Oh, sweetheart, you're not a ho." Gabrielle smoothed Shoshanna's red hair back. "You're *the* ho. I hail to the ho." She pretended to bow.

"Quit making me laugh. You're evil to make me laugh. It hurts."

Gabrielle struggled to stay positive, but she wanted to cry seeing her friend hospitalized. "I can't understand how that wheel came off like that. I keep thinking about it."

"Don't blame yourself, Gabby. Kitchen accidents happen. They call it occupational hazard." Shoshanna sighed. "My mother wants me to quit cooking, period. She thinks it'll kill me, but I told her that if I can't go back to cooking, *that'll* kill me. Cooking is my life."

"I understand."

"I knew you wouldn't think I'm crazy."

"So what are you facing?"

"The leg shouldn't need more surgery, if it heals well. The burns? Skin grafting."

"Skin grafting? As in taking skin from some other part of your body and putting it where the burns are?"

"Yeah, but the transplantation's only for the third-degree area. The burn on my arm's going to scar, but I'm thinking about covering it with a tattoo down the line."

"Tattoos aren't so bad."

"I know. You have just the one, right?"

"Yup. Just the dandelion."

"Gabby, why are you so sad? You're sadder today than you were when you visited me all those other times. What's going on?"

"More weirdness at the restaurant," she said. "Fridges mysteriously unplugging themselves and costing us big dollars. Yesterday Stu opened a cabinet and wineglasses fell out in a sheet of glass. I witnessed that. My heart jumped into my throat—I thought he might've been seriously injured, but thank God he'd only had a few superficial cuts."

"How is he?"

"Oh, a couple of bandages and he was back to cooking. But still… I don't know, Shosh. You've seen *The Wizard of Oz*, right? Know that part where the lion insists he doesn't believe in spooks until they're attacked in the woods and then he changes his mind real fast?"

"Gabby, are you telling me you believe in the curse of the Belleza?"

"Not exactly. But I believe someone *wants* me to. Someone is behind all of this hell and I want to find them."

"Damn, you're a scrapper."

"Well, my team's being targeted and I have to protect you all."

"Any guesses? Who would want to sabotage us? The fire and the wineglasses sound like intent to maim or kill."

"And tampering with equipment, such as a kitchen cart."

Shoshanna swallowed. "My accident?"

"Maybe the intent wasn't to get you specifically, but someone was bound to get hurt dealing with that messed up wheel." Gabrielle smoothed her hair again. "You're safer here, Shosh. But I'm going to find out who's responsible for hurting you and I'm going to make sure they pay."

The woman's smile wobbled. "You're always out to protect everyone else. Who's looking out for you?"

"The Belleza has my back. There's Kim and Robyn and Jonah and Stu. Stu's been trying to get me out of the kitchen, actually. He suggested I go to a club and meet someone."

"Well, you must. Remember what I told you? The next sexy man—"

"Oh, about that. I did meet a sexy man, and I almost hooked up with him the other night."

Shoshanna's expression shifted from worried to curious. "Who is he? How *could* you not tell me sooner?"

"All right, but I'm only telling you my dirty dark secrets because you're stuck in the hospital and I know I can trust you to keep this on the low."

"Tell me."

Gabrielle shut the hospital room door and reclaimed her seat. "His name's Geoffrey Girard." She unburdened herself, confessing how far she and Geoffrey had gone that night at the Pearl and that in a couple of days she would be joining him on a jet to his hot springs retreat.

"Gabby, it doesn't seem like Kim or Robyn or anyone else would think less of you for dating this man," Shoshanna said. "You're pulling yourself back and I'm trying to understand your position, but I don't. I don't know why you're denying yourself this chance."

"Did I not mention that he has a history as a serial dater?"

"So what? You haven't exactly been a one-man kind of woman, right? It's the twenty-first century. Most people have romantic pasts. I think you're on a fishing expedition, trying to catch reasons to push him away."

"You're medicated. I'll forgive you for that."

"Bull and you know it. I just want you to understand that you deserve to be protected and happy as much as the rest of us. Find out if Geoffrey's a man who can protect you and make you happy, and if he is, please don't be an asshole about it."

Gabrielle twisted her mouth. "At first, I thought *he* was the asshole."

"Seems he's a lot like you. I want to meet him. Don't alienate this man before I have a chance to meet him." Shoshanna closed her eyes. "Leave me alone now. I'm tired."

Sighing, Gabrielle stood up. Shoshanna cracked open an eye. "Got any candy bars on you? Snickers? TWIX?"

"A granola bar."

"Leave me alone."

Gabrielle grinned, patting her shoulder. "Thanks for the talk, Shosh."

"Y'all sure you can survive without me for two days?"

It was Friday and in roughly an hour Gabrielle was expected at Geoffrey's Beverly Hills mansion to drive them to his private jet. She couldn't get Shoshanna's advice out of her head, and that combined with her friends' well-meaning intent to see her dating someone and her own boiling attraction to Geoffrey was building to a volatile point. Now she was isolating herself with him.

"We're sure," Robyn insisted.

Kim, who'd had a gourmet breakfast delivered to the pool where they sat around a table, looked around and divulged, "I'm taking measures to get to the truth about what's going on here."

Robyn picked up an orange slice. "What sort of measures?"

"A PI."

"PI? An investigator?"

"Yes. As strange and albeit supernatural as these problems appear, I think it's a ruse and someone's out to destroy the place my family built. Well, I'm not going to let that happen."

Gabrielle sipped her cranberry juice. "Any leads?"

"My parents reminded me that the Pinnacle is our direct competition."

The Pinnacle was a new hotel that had opened its doors barely a half hour's drive from the Belleza Resort. "Good thinking, Kurt and Ilene," Gabrielle said of Kim's parents. "We've been top dog here and the Pinnacle naturally wants some of the attention. A business's first year is often its most crucial."

"I think it's too obvious. Not to mention too sloppy," Robyn said. "Eventually the obvious suspect would be the Pinnacle. You'd think a new establishment would want to keep its hands clean of any traces. Directly harming folks over here? That's not clean."

"Well, we can't afford to *not* suspect the Pinnacle," Kim reasoned. "Another track to consider is that one of our own is involved."

"What the hell? Someone on our staff?" Gabrielle couldn't entertain the thought, but the indignation lasted for only a minute. Money motivated people to adopt uncharacteristic behavior. Money turned friends into enemies. Money could be a tool for good or for evil. "Set a fire, unplug a fridge, for what? A clear shot to a treasure that no one really knows even exists? Seems utterly stupid. Anyone who tries to cash in on this so-called treasure would be suspected."

"There's more than those incidents, Gabby." Kim leaned forward. "There's been theft. Electronic stuff, missing from guests' rooms. A full-blown rash of theft and the only thing that makes sense is that someone who has access to guests' suites is taking advantage."

"I heard that someone had sneaked into the Pearl last week," Robyn said.

Gabrielle dropped her fork onto her plate. "Uh— what?"

The guard had given her his discretion. He'd reneged?

"I didn't get a report on that." Kim sat straight, looking every bit the strong and capable leader that she'd always been. "What details do you have?"

"Not much. It was spa gossip. All I know is someone was there after it closed for the night. Maybe this is connected to the theft and everything else that's going on."

"How come you didn't tell me before now?" Kim asked.

"I apologize, but it was only a suspicion. No proof, and Gabby, nothing's come up missing, has it?"

My common sense. She'd had no good reason to sneak into the Pearl with Geoffrey and to get hot and heavy with him in the kitchen where she worked every day. Shoshanna knew her secrets, but it didn't seem enough to still hide the truth from her best friends. "No, nothing's missing. We check inventory regularly. My staff's on high alert."

"Good." But Kim still didn't appear relaxed.

"You'd better get back to the condo, Gabby," Robyn said. "Let yourself have a good time and try not to worry about the Belleza. Kim and I can hold things down."

Grateful for an excuse to escape the table and her guilt, Gabrielle took an orange slice and got up. "If you need me—"

"We won't need you. Have fun out there in an oasis with the sexiest music producer ever. Lucky woman."

Forcing a laugh, it was all Gabrielle could do to walk and not run from the friends she'd lied to.

Chapter 7

Gabrielle made up her mind, staring down the suitcases next to her door. She would *not* be having sex. Eventually she might—she hoped, at least—but it wouldn't happen while she was on a working weekend in Storey Springs, California. She couldn't be more prepared to meet Geoffrey's guests. Excitement mingled with nervousness, and the more she repeated in her head that this was strictly a business trip, the more she didn't believe it.

The brand new undies she'd packed despite the celibacy vow she'd made to herself was proof.

Just as she impulsively grabbed one of her bags to take out the undies and leave them in the condo, the bell rang. A pair of panties in hand, she hurried to the door.

Stu came in, shrinking the place with his big lumberjack build. His hair was freshly highlighted and he appraised her critically through those classically Stu, thick fuchsia frames. "I'm about to start my shift at the restaurant and thought I'd say bon voyage first, Chef Royce." He frowned at the underwear in her hand. "What are those?"

"Women's undies."

"Lord, I know what they are. I mean to say, what are you doing running around with them?"

"I'm changing my underwear. The underwear I packed for this trip. The luggage is full of sexy panties and stuff, and this trip isn't about that."

Stu rubbed his forehead. "Does it matter what kind of underwear you're packing? Who's going to see it?"

"That's the problem."

"How so? Oh, because you're wanting the host with the most to see your vixen panties."

Gabrielle nodded. "That's kind of it exactly."

"Put the underwear back in your suitcase and let's go. Pretty soon you're going to talk yourself out of the whole damn thing and I was planning to tear up the streets without you being all lonely and sad and sex-deprived and making me feel guilty about it."

"You saying I drag you down, Chef Merritt?"

"I'm saying that for the past couple of weeks, I've been more concerned about finding you a man than finding myself one. *No me gusto.*"

As Gabrielle locked up behind her and walked with Stu to the parking garage, she said, "The trip was going to happen, despite the underwear drama. I'm just having trouble keeping things in check."

"You're so effing adorable like this, Gabby. You're like the way you were when he first came into the kitchen at the Pearl and pissed you off. But now there's more. You look gratified. Like you won the lottery jackpot or had great sex. Did you gamble?"

Getting involved with Geoffrey was a gamble with higher stakes than she could afford to risk. "No."

Stu turned to her. "Chef Royce, did you have sex?"

"No. But we kissed."

"You kissed? When and why am I just now hearing about it?"

"I don't have time to get into the particulars, but it was good and unfortunately can't happen again."

"Why not? Isn't he what you want? Besides the sexual pull, there's something more to you and Geoffrey, isn't there?" he asked gently. "How will I do my duty as a helpful friend if you won't let me? Talk."

"The kiss wasn't enough for me, even though it's got to be. I still feel a little bit unfulfilled, if you understand what I mean. Sex would unbelievable—hot, passionate, wild, reckless. But insanely, I want more than even that. I like being around him, talking to him, letting him charm me even if my reasonable mind says it's wrong."

"Tell your reasonable mind I said STFU."

At her truck, she loaded her luggage and hugged him. "Try not to be too lax in the kitchen while I'm gone. When I get back, we're all going to work harder. It's going to be balls to the wall."

"I know that's an expression and all, but I have balls and that just sounds painful to me."

Snorting a laugh, she got into the truck and activated the GPS, feeling better about the weekend ahead.

That buoyancy sank when she arrived at Geoffrey's gated mansion and saw the flare of temptation in his eyes. One kiss was a tease. It was cruelty.

I'm either going to survive this trip by pretending

*that there's nothing between us, or I'm going to have
him naked before we get to the tarmac.*

"This will be your suite."

Gabrielle followed a maid into a stadium of a room
that had a hall that opened to more rooms. The place
was decorated in gentle colors and rich fabrics and
sleek, modern furniture. The windows introduced her
to a view of jungle-like trees and plants. "It's beautiful."

"What can I get for you?"

"Nothing. It's beautiful," she said again, mesmer-
ized. She and Geoffrey had arrived a while ago, but
they'd had lunch at a café before a driver had brought
them to the oasis. An oasis, it was. Cool air, luscious
scenery, acres of quiet tranquility.

"If you think of anything, page me." The maid handed
her a card with her contact information on it.

Gabrielle's first order of business was a relaxing
bath. The oversized claw-foot tub cradled her in fragrant bubbles and she was so soothed that she climbed
out of the tub and fell into a dreamless sleep on the
neatly made bed. Darkness had fallen by the time
she awoke and rolled off the bed. Leaving the windows open to the summer breeze, she got dressed and
checked her smartphone.

A text from Kim.

Stop obsessing about the Belleza. I know you are.

One from Robyn.

If you don't let yourself meet someone on this trip,
I'm setting you up with someone when you get back.

P.S. I hate blind dates, so don't think about retaliating in kind. Luv you!

Gabrielle was a confident enough explorer to not require the maid's help in finding her way around the main house. There were several outbuildings and she figured she'd enjoy the journey more if she checked them out in daylight. Walking through the numerous halls, glancing into glorious room after glorious room, she began to feel overwhelmed. It was more extravagant than anything she'd ever seen. Her family was certainly well-to-do, but their wealth couldn't compare to that of a man who owned an oasis the size of a moderately sized city.

"What do you think?"

"Geoffrey. Hey." She smiled. He wasn't this place. He was deeper than his riches. She wanted the man, not the money. "I was about to call out 'Marco' and see if you answered 'Polo.'"

"So are you liking what you see here?"

"I like you," she said honestly. When he frowned a little, she explained, "I appreciate that you're sharing your private space with me. And I'm ready to meet everyone else."

"Not everyone is here, but most of them are. A couple of producers, some of my clients and their guests. Phenom's here."

"I have orders to secure an autograph for our songbird Charlene." To be completely truthful, Charlene had begged Gabrielle to pass along her business card to the performer, but Gabrielle already knew *that* wasn't going to happen. It wasn't in the best taste and it seemed an underhanded move to make when Geoffrey had already told the woman that he wouldn't do it.

"She doesn't want the autograph on one of her business cards, does she?"

"She didn't specify," Gabrielle said carefully. Why she constantly sheltered the woman from her own errors baffled her. Perhaps she felt sorry for Charlene. Or it had everything to do with their similarities. "Where is everyone?"

"Come on."

He brought her to a studio inside the main house. She knew there was a separate wood-fronted building that housed his private recording studio, and according to him it was hardly used, since he didn't sing professionally.

That nugget of info turned into a full anecdote when they entered the sleek recording studio and one of the guests played a bone-meltingly seductive R&B ballad and outed Geoffrey as the artist.

"That's *you*?" she whispered, searching his eyes as the song wound around her again and again.

"Yeah. I was in my twenties and thought about performing, but I'd rather produce records and let folks like them have the stage." He sent a menacing look to the man playing the track. "You got an ass-kicking coming."

"Could you let the song finish before you kick his ass? I like it." She drew him into a slow sway. "I've heard of actors who prefer to never watch their finished work and authors who refuse to read their own published books, but never of musicians who don't listen to their own songs."

"Now you've heard of one." But Geoffrey didn't

stop dancing with her. "I'm only letting this play because you want it to, Gabrielle."

"I'm a guest. You have to give me what I want. It's a rule."

"Really?"

"In this case it is."

The song faded and she let him lead her around the room. It buzzed with expensively dressed people. Vintage guitars were mounted on one wall, and after introductions and some mingling with Phenom Jones's girlfriend, who'd recognized Gabrielle's name from her recent "The Hottest Kitchens in California" interview published in one of the country's most popular entertainment magazines, she gravitated to the instruments. Behind her, she could hear Geoffrey requesting pricey liquor for his guests and the staff politely and promptly fulfilling those requests. No luxury had been spared, and she kept coming back to the thought that this oasis wasn't the Geoffrey she knew. Which was the real man, she didn't know. It burned her up that she even gave a damn. After July, he'd have no reason to cross her path and he would realize that he liked what was familiar: women who made themselves appear perfect and who were manipulated by wealth.

Was that the real reason he'd invited her here? To find out if he could mold her with his money?

Offended at the thought, she continued to look at the guitars.

"Gabby, you've been looking at those guitars so long you must've picked a favorite by now," he said.

She whipped around. "Don't call me Gabby. My friends call me Gabby. Not men who want to get me naked."

A moment ago the control room had pulsed with a chorus of male voices and a harmony of deep male laughter. Now it was silent, and, turning her back to the blue-lighted guitar case, Gabrielle forgot about autographs and auctions and vintage instruments altogether.

Geoffrey sat relaxed in a plush leather chair, his body still except for the tap of his finger on the glass paperweight on the desk. The item probably cost five figures, easy. He kept his receptionists in diamonds and his guests in limousines. He'd had a recording studio built on a man-made hot spring. Of course he'd spare no expense to furnish the place.

The tapping mimicked the rhythm of her heartbeat, and when he suddenly stopped, she imagined her heart skipped its next beat. "I didn't say I wanted to get you naked."

"You didn't have to. A lot of times, it's what men say *without* words that counts." Gabrielle walked past the men occupying the leather sofas and women holding crystal serving trays, not giving any of them the benefit of intimidation. She'd been raised in this world, and had fought hard to never let it control her. She rounded the consoles and mixers and stood in front of Geoffrey. She wouldn't let his heartbreaking sexiness and her crazy thirst for him intimidate her, either. "You brought me to this billion-dollar oasis to show me that the music world thinks you're a god. But, Geoffrey, that doesn't impress me. Money hasn't impressed me for a long time."

"Good," he said, still sitting so relaxed. Calm. Watching and waiting. Baiting, really. "I'm not going to get you naked. You're going to get yourself naked. And when you do, it's not going to be because you want my money. It's going to be because you want *me*."

Gabrielle slowly took in their audience, then the seriousness on Geoffrey's face. And she laughed.

A few other people chuckled uncertainly, as though they weren't sure whether to join in on the laughter or continue to watch with their mouths shut.

Geoffrey stood and then her hand was in his and they were moving toward the control room. She ended up in the lone chair and he was before her, his expression honest and tortured.

"I know you don't want my money," he said.

There were people on the other side of the booth, she knew it. But she couldn't get herself to tear away from his gaze or the intense invisible hold he had on her. This wasn't completely her choice. He had a say in what happened between them, too. For the first time, she was truly realizing that.

"I don't know that you want me," he finished.

"I do."

"Show me."

Gabrielle pushed his chest and wouldn't let go until his back was to the wall. Her palms flattened on the wall, framing his head, and when he bent to bring his face to hers, she stretched up kissed him with a force she didn't know she possessed. She didn't know her tongue could be so greedy. She didn't know her hands could be so demanding. She didn't know she could bear the press of his cock against her belly.

"You," she moaned. "It's just you I want. It was never about your money. It never will be. Get it now?"

"When we go back, I want the chance to show you it doesn't have to be about money. Let me prove I'm not trying to buy you. Give me that chance before you decide whether you want to be with me or not."

She thought she said okay, but the word was shattered in a kiss.

"Don't take this the wrong way, Gabby, but you look awful. Didn't you just come back from a vacation upstate?"

Gabrielle scowled at her assistant but didn't respond because she'd heard similar comments in the Belleza's main lobby, in the elevator and at the coffee machine near her office. "I pulled an all-nighter, but it was well worth it. I've developed a menu for the Dunham Foundation for a Better Future gala and want to run it by Kim and Robyn and Jaxon this afternoon. You're more than welcome to join us, too."

"Sounds good." Roarke shuffled through a scatter of papers on his desk. "Geoffrey Girard stopped by not too long ago. He said he wanted to confirm dinner on Thursday and to either call his assistant or his cell if you need anything. Don't contact him at his office because he has an interview this morning." He handed over a Post-it that had the same information and said, "Um, it's not my business, but are you seeing him?"

Gabrielle's mouth fell agape. "No," she said, unexplainably flustered at the question. "Dinner tomorrow night is just a business thing," she said, not exactly sure if that was so.

"You've been doing a lot of business things with him that don't include any of the staff, though. Again, not my business."

"Why are you keeping at this, then, Roarke?"

"Since when is it a problem if I ask? We talk about this stuff, don't we?"

"I don't know. I had to hear from Charlene that you and your girlfriend broke up in June. Why didn't you tell me? I would've inducted you into the Lonely Hearts Society." She suddenly recalled Geoffrey's accusation that Roarke was nursing a crush on her, and she dreaded to ask her next question. "Is this about you and me, Roarke?"

"What's 'you and me,' exactly, Gabby? Define that."

"We're friends. Colleagues."

"Yeah," he said, dragging out the word. Disappointment dripped from every letter. "Friends. Colleagues. It's not like you invite me into the Pearl after closing."

Oh. Lord. No. "What?"

Roarke held her shocked stare. Smug satisfaction was a look she'd never associate with him, but there it was. "I know your habits better than you do. On top of that, I'm not a freaking idiot. I know it was you in the Pearl that night and I have this feeling that the man who was with you is the same one who's bringing you gourmet lunches and taking you on trips."

Two days ago, Geoffrey had come to her office with a delicious lunch that he'd prepared himself and afterward he'd taken her on a sunset Hummer tour of the Mojave Desert. That night he'd poured her wine and they'd ended up reading passages from *Of Mice and Men.*

It had been one of the most spectacular dates of her life and it hadn't been about money or status. It had been just Geoffrey and Gabrielle.

"Um…oh…well, he said you were invited, too, but I didn't think the Pearl could spare us both."

"Like I'd want to watch you with him? No, thanks." Roarke set his hands down on top of the desk. "Just tell me the truth, okay? Were you two in the Pearl that night? Kim Parker's ready to fire the security on watch that night for not doing their jobs, and if you have information that'd save their jobs, you need to quit covering your ass if you want to save theirs."

Gabrielle closed her eyes. "Damn it. This is so messed up."

"It was you, wasn't it?"

"Yes. We were talking about menu options for his company's gala—"

"If that's all it was, why didn't you tell anyone before now?"

"That's not all it was. A guard came into the kitchen and saw us kissing." She barely noticed the muscle leap in Roarke's neck. "He said he'd keep quiet about it but there's been talk and everyone's on edge. Do you think when I tell Kim that she's going to ask me to resign?"

Her assistant shrugged as if to say you never know. "I have this buddy who was fired while he was on his honeymoon in Cancun." Roarke must have noticed the stunned and alarmed look that crossed her face because he backpedaled with, "Kim's stressed but not insane. I'd say your job is safe, but you should take care of this before someone else tells her first. Some people just tune out the facts and sop up the gossip."

"Roarke, about Geoffrey and me. Does that offend you in any way?"

"Why would I be offended? We're friends and colleagues."

"I didn't notice that you thought about me that way. If I had—"

"What, you'd let me take you out? Or would we sneak around the way you and he are?"

"Neither. We could've talked it out so no one's feelings would end up hurt."

"Well, no need for that now. Just talk to Kim and find somewhere else to hold your midnight meetings while our company's under attack."

Stung, Gabrielle said nothing more. She texted Kim that she needed to talk to her before she fired anyone, and Kim responded that she was out of town on business until tomorrow night. Then, before she made it to her truck in the parking lot, she got a call from Robyn.

"You're going on a date tonight. There'll be no time to linger in the kitchen, because you're meeting a man named Tom Ward in Hollywood. He's a friend of a friend of a friend of a… You get the point."

"A blind date? I thought you were joking."

"No, ma'am. You made nothing of your trip to Storey Springs. So I'm pulling you off the shelf."

"No, leave me on the shelf. It's comfortable."

"Gabrielle, you're doing this. We'll talk about everything later. I have a meeting but wanted to catch you before you took on another double shift at the Pearl."

When Robyn hung up, Gabrielle almost hit her smartphone against her head. Kim was on a firing rampage, Robyn was finding blind dates and neither of them would be doing that if Gabrielle had just been honest with them from the get-go. She wasn't someone who stuck to her convictions. She was a coward and she was a hypocrite and she was starting to picture a future with Geoffrey.

But she and Geoffrey wouldn't work out, not after the truth came to light about what they'd done in the

Pearl. She'd judged the hostess for singing in the restaurant, but at least Charlene hadn't sneaked around. Gabrielle didn't like the version of herself who lied to save her own skin.

Something had to give.

In Beverly Hills, she arrived at G&G Records and power-walked down a hushed, immaculate hallway. Soon she was standing at his assistant's desk.

"Mr. Girard is preparing for an interview," the glamorous assistant said. She clicked on a screen on her computer and said, "I can put you in at the end of the—"

"That won't do," she interrupted firmly. "I have an urgent matter to discuss with him. I'll be brief. Pick up the phone and tell him I'm on the way in." With that, she marched across the outer office and pushed open his door.

He turned to her with confused eyes, then held up a finger and picked up the ringing phone. "Yes, Cathy. Actually, she's standing right in front of me. Thank you." With a headshake, he disconnected and summoned her in with a hitch of his chin. He rose from his chair and rounded a polished mahogany desk to approach her. His gaze coasted over her and he commented, "You seem tense this morning. Didn't sleep well?"

It wasn't easy to remain livid with him with those primitive wishful thoughts of him moving naked on top of her creeping into her mind. She hoped her skin didn't flush. "Um, as a matter of fact, I'm low on rest but high on productivity." He nodded and hinted at a smile. He slid his hands in his pockets and prompted,

"So, what's the emergency? I'm due for an interview soon, so we should probably make this quick."

"What is it that you're after?" she demanded. At his puzzled expression, she clarified, "I'm talking about the kisses and the gourmet lunch and the Hummer tour and *Of Mice and Men* and the fact that you're pursuing me as if I'm important to you."

"You are important to me. As for everything else you listed, that's just me spending time with you."

"Do you know what I'm sacrificing to spend time with you? My integrity. I'm lying to my friends and my coworkers and myself. The guard who saw us kissing in the kitchen that night? He might be fired, all because of my feelings for you. I didn't bank on all this trouble. It's too much."

"Can't a Belleza client show his appreciation to the fantastic staff?"

"Not when the client is you and the staff is me." She studied him, struck by the adjective he'd used to describe her. "Do you seriously think I'm fantastic?"

Geoffrey's hand reached out as if he wanted to touch her, but he changed his mind and said, "Gabrielle, I think you have a problem believing compliments. It's not that you don't believe in yourself. It's apparent that you do. But you don't think others believe in you."

"Confidence is one thing. Results another."

His phone intruded and he swiped it up. When he hung up from the call, he said, "Interview time. Look, I'm not interested in taking the fall for your lying to everyone. If you think I should back off, tell me that."

"I'm going on a date. Tonight. It's a blind date that one of my friends set up. She did that because she thinks I'm lonely. She doesn't know about you and me. See how freakin' complicated this is?"

"Go on the date. I'm going to be at Club Groove in Hollywood for a business dinner. It's casual but something I need to do."

"You're not threatened?"

"No."

"Why don't you care more than that? Why don't you give a damn that I might like this guy?"

"You might like him, but you feel something stronger for me. I know you do. So no, I'm not threatened. Got no reason to be."

"Great, then. I'm going on a date with someone else. And after this, I'm done lying to my colleagues and my friends. I have to be honest."

He looked at her with respect and admiration. "You're real. That's what I love most about you."

"Don't say that word. As of this second, I'm blanking out that you said that word."

"Go ahead and try. If you've never failed at anything before, you will if you think you can forget what I said."

Life had lovely days and sucky ones. Today was a sucky one. Gabrielle and Geoffrey were both in Hollywood, but while he was at the hip Club Groove, she was stuck at a bar-and-grill having dinner with a man Robyn knew through mutual friends. Tom Ward had called her and asked her to dress nicely, and so she had, not expecting to be taken to a cramped place with so much humidity that her hair immediately had begun to frizz the moment she stepped in.

Now, as she unenthusiastically stabbed at her medium rare hamburger and pretended to be enthralled in Tom Ward's business investments, she wished that she'd had the guts to decline the blind date.

Robyn had meant well. She didn't know that Gabrielle had all the man she could ask for in Geoffrey Girard.

"Some people say they have hunches about which stocks to invest in," Tom was saying in between bites of a greasy hot dog loaded with the works. If he hadn't had mustard on his chin and wasn't boring her senseless with his business talk, he would've been incredibly handsome. "Relying on hunches is too risky for me," he continued. "I study the stock market, use my brain. As a side note, it's rumored that the brain is in fact the sexiest organ of the body."

Gabrielle's already lazy appetite rolled over and died. She inconspicuously checked the time on her cell phone that she'd positioned on the booth beside her. Was it polite to end dinner with someone after twenty-five minutes?

Tom polished off his meal and looked at her full plate. "Is the burger too rare, Gabrielle? I'll have the waitress send it back—"

"No, don't trouble yourself."

Tom wiped his face with a napkin, catching the mustard smear. He said congenially to her, "You've certainly become successful. Executive Chef is a mighty title. And you're a twenty-eight-year-old master chef on top of that? It helps to have a nudge from family, doesn't it?"

"Absolutely," she said with annoyance, "but hard work and genuine talent sustain my career, Tom."

"Right." He cleared his throat and considered her.

"I did stumble upon something in the paper the other week that mentioned some troubles at the Pearl, though. Health hazards?"

She couldn't quite figure out if he was genuinely concerned or was screwing with her. "The Pearl's recovered from similar troubles in the past. We have no reason to believe it'd be any different now."

"Come on, though. Put in a fine woman as general manager, put you in as executive chef… Obviously the owners are hoping a few beautiful faces will be their aces. But how long will that sustain a business that's vulnerable to theft and mysterious incidents? The customers are going to go where they feel safe, not where they need to constantly hang on to their valuables or look up every other second wondering if a piano's going to drop out of the sky like in some old cartoon."

Her jaw twitched. He made sense, but his point was buried in disdain. "The Parkers didn't hire beautiful faces to cover up crappy business management. Every member of the Belleza team is qualified for their job. We won't buckle because someone's trying to edge us out of the market."

Tom picked up his beer. "Fight to the end. Guess I admire that. But if you want my opinion, the Parkers should sell the entire resort and let someone take it in an entirely new direction."

"Someone? Or perhaps a development firm? Are you sitting here because you're legitimately interested in a date, or are you here to broker a deal?" When he didn't say anything, she swore. "I could sniff out your ulterior motive, Tom. I don't appreciate you using me to get information to feed some developer, and I doubt Robyn would appreciate it, either."

"Who says this isn't a date? You shouldn't be hung up on preconceptions based on my line of work. I could sit here and accuse you of having dinner with me because you want an excuse to brush up on the local cuisine to better your own craft. See where I'm taking this? Now be fair and give me a chance."

She said nothing.

"Are you looking for a long-term relationship?" he asked.

"I don't view dating like that—the means to marriage. I prefer to enjoy spending time with someone and then see what develops. Pushing things helps no one. What about you?"

"I'm more traditional. Robyn told me your grandmother was an accomplished equestrian. You share her love for horses?" It surprised her that Robyn had told him so much backstory. Her grandmother May had been a horse trainer. One of her horses had gone to the Kentucky Derby. She'd visited the equestrian center only once, for a summer, and it had been one of the tensest summers of her life.

Gabrielle must've slipped away into the memories because Tom reached to touch her hand. "Sorry. I was thinking about something. To answer your question, I'm a fair rider, but don't have the gift."

"You could get out of the kitchen and dabble in riding or some other hobbies, distance yourself from the Belleza when the real hell hits. I can sense it's going to happen. Spare yourself."

"Excuse me?"

"You're angry," he said. "Calm down."

"No, I love when people use me for business manipulation," she said sarcastically. She slapped down a twenty-dollar bill and slid out of the booth.

He quickly rose and caught her arm. "Please don't leave angry, Gabrielle," he pleaded. "I wanted this to be a nice date for us."

"May I be honest with you?" she said, whirling. "I only agreed to have dinner with you out of respect to Robyn. I don't plan to ever see you again."

In her haste out the door, she crashed into Roarke. "Where's the fire?" he said, stilling her.

"*Why* do people say that? There is no fire." Relaying her evening with him was not something she felt up to at the moment. "I'm just in a hurry."

"Where to?"

"Home," she said. Then she noticed that he was clean-shaven, wearing a new button-down shirt and cologne. "Are you on a date?"

He nodded. "A paralegal. Blonde, brown-eyed, slim as a flute. She's from Sacramento and I've been giving her tours of the city."

I'll just bet.

"Hope your night turns out better than mine did."

"See you at work."

"Okay." She paused. "Hey, we're okay, aren't we?"

"We're okay."

As she drove through the dark night aimlessly, she tried to be happy for her assistant. It was good that he was attracted to someone else. As long as the paralegal kept him distracted, she wouldn't feel guilty about her feelings for Geoffrey.

A vision of Geoffrey's body moving over hers clouded her mind, and she hooked an immediate left at the intersection, knowing exactly where she wanted to be: with him.

She knew where to find him. She knew what she was after.

What she didn't know was what tomorrow would be like if they made love tonight.

Gabrielle's subtle curves felt good under Geoffrey's hands. "What is this you have on?" he muttered against her throat as he squeezed her booty and ran his fingers over the material.

She had come to him at Club Groove, where she'd known he would be while she was somewhere else on a date. They had made it to his car in the club's parking lot and now she was draped over his hard lap.

"Stretch silk," she sighed, her head thrown back to allow his mouth access to the hollow between her collarbones.

"God bless stretch silk." He breathed in her light perfume and licked at her skin as his fingers moved under her hemline. His palms cruised up her slender thighs and searched for the lacy straps of the thong he knew she had on beneath that skintight dress.

She tensed and rocked back. "Wait."

Oh, hell, that really wasn't the word he was expecting. He stilled, though, and looked at her through the shadowy darkness. Most likely she had reservations about going at it in a car practically in public. He could understand and respect that. Trying to not dwell on the blood pounding in his crotch, he said, "Do you want to book a room?"

She shook her head and brushed her wild hair from her face. "That's not what I mean. We shouldn't have sex. I'm sorry to do this to you, but I have to be sensible. I came here tonight because once again I wanted to have sex with you and also because I simply wanted to *be* with you."

He didn't pretend to understand where she was going with this. All he knew was that after settling business with promoters and clients, tossing back a few nonalcoholic drinks and enjoying the atmosphere, his night had been topped when he saw Gabrielle enter the bar looking gorgeous in her dress and high heels.

But, now that he thought about it, she'd seemed a little disconcerted.

"What happened tonight?"

"It's not your problem, and really, it's so insignificant. He and I just don't mesh. I tried to keep an open mind for my friend's sake, but I basically told him that I'd rather not see his face again." Again she hesitated. "But that's not why I'm not going to sleep with you tonight."

"Why, then?" He flexed his hips under her.

She sucked in a breath. "You're making this harder."

"I should be saying that to you."

"Geoffrey."

His head dropped back against the headrest. "Sorry."

"We're taking this too fast. We need a breather from each other and to think like rational adults about what sort of arrangement this will be. Am I just a piece of ass to you?"

"No," he said immediately. "I can't believe you even asked me that question."

She snorted. "I almost wish the answer was yes. Then it'd be more difficult to become dependent on you. After this blind date gone wrong, I came instantly to you. Don't you see what this is all leading to?"

"We're not in a relationship."

"This feels like one. What's happening between us is more than curiosity. Do you agree?"

Geoffrey nodded but didn't totally agree. Yes, he was crazy with curiosity about what it'd feel like to be inside her, to make her moan and twist in pleasure. But once he had her, he wouldn't be lulled with the thought of not having her again.

That wasn't good. He didn't have addictions, and he'd make damn sure that Gabrielle Royce didn't become his first.

He tucked his shirt into his pants and said, "You've made some very good points, and I apologize again for getting my back up about you being with that guy. I don't have the right to weigh in on who you have dinner with or even sleep with."

He heard her exhale deeply. She cleared her throat and replied, "Yeah, that's the best way to categorize things. We're not exclusive by any means."

He had a loophole, was free to go to someone else, so why was he so reluctant to take it? "Gabrielle…"

She fumbled for her keys. "Listen, call me the second you have a confirmed guest list. If anyone's willing to divulge their food allergies, we'd appreciate the information. I'll call Robyn and Roarke in the morning and make sure we're on track."

"Gabrielle," he said again, his voice both harsh and gentle. What sort of spell did she have him under where he couldn't even let her get out of his car without kissing her again? When he snagged her attention and she leaned forward, he pulled her into a thorough kiss.

And she responded automatically, curling her fingers into his sleeves and parting her mouth for him. His hand was shooting up her thigh before he could stop the motion. Once he encountered her underwear, he broke the kiss and said, "Tell me what to do next. You want control, right? Take it."

"Put your hand on me. Move the thong out of the way."

Obeying, he had his fingers inside her quick. The friction built as she rode his hand and he watched, selfishly taking pleasure in the knowledge that he was the one who made her speechless with arousal.

As her orgasm crested, she rocked onto his hand and hit his shoulders, but he wouldn't stop until he felt her walls grip around his fingers and heard his name fall from her lips.

Silence followed, until she finally crawled off his lap and flopped back against the passenger seat. "My God. I came in a Bugatti."

What would they do when the gala was over and there was nothing to keep them apart?

Chapter 8

"A clairvoyant."

Gabrielle waited for Kimberly's reaction as they sat in the parlor of the Parker family's splendid Spanish Colonial estate. Kimberly had been so busy upon her return to Belleza that she hadn't given Gabrielle an opportunity to confess anything before now. Kurt and Ilene Parker were hosting a casual dinner at home, and Gabrielle couldn't decline on account of she was overflowing with guilt.

The Parkers' estate was only a few miles from the resort, but for Gabrielle the drive had taken an eternity to complete. Every second inched up her dread, because she knew what she'd have to do. She would have to put on her big girl panties and cop to what she'd done. She had made a mistake and didn't believe the security who'd given her discretion when she'd all but begged for it deserved to lose employment based on her lapse in judgment.

Robyn was there, as was Kimberly's fiancé, Jaxon Dunham. Jaxon, the heir to the Dunham fortune, was too suave for words and though Gabrielle's clothes weren't too shabby, she felt underdressed whenever she was in the same room as he. Conversation had been smooth yet tense. Everyone had the same thing on their mind: the string of kooky incidents. Yet no one had broached the subject until Gabrielle had said, "People are still talking about a so-called hex on the resort. I think that if the majority believes in this, the best solution would be to recruit a clairvoyant."

"A what?" Kimberly had responded.

And now they faced each other and Kimberly was slightly shaking her head as though to gauge whether or not Gabrielle was kidding her.

"You're not serious right now," Kimberly decided.

"I am. I've already contacted one. Her name is Annie."

"What?" Robyn chimed in. "A clairvoyant named Annie? Don't know, it just seems she'd be named something more…mystical."

"This one is supposed to be the real deal. She's been on TV—"

"Ah, there's your gold standard," Kimberly cut in.

"In documentaries, I was going to add. She's published books, has impressive research credentials. *I* don't believe there's a real curse, but when in Rome…"

"We're not in Rome," Robyn said. "We're in California and I know there have been reports of paranormal activity across the country, I'd hold off on calling Annie the Clairvoyant. What do you think, Kurt? Ilene?"

Kimberly's mother sat on a plush armchair. "I think there are too many unknowns to make smart accusations."

"Which is why I have a different solution. One a bit less woo-woo." Kim faced her parents. "I've hired a private investigator. He's already scoped things out and reported back to me some findings. Unfortunately for us, he doesn't see a connection between the fire and the fake reviews and the kitchen mishaps. He thinks it's all coincidental. Odd, but coincidental."

"How does that help us out?"

"Maybe it's peace of mind, if you want it," Kimberly suggested. "If not for the staff, then at least for the guests. We don't want droves of people canceling reservations. It could kill our business."

That made Gabrielle think that someone wanted such a result. With the Belleza folded, someone would profit. "Someone has an ax to grind deep."

Robyn jerked, and while Jaxon checked if she was okay, Gabrielle glanced at her, brow furrowed. Why was she on edge?

"What came of your look into that incident at the Pearl?" Jaxon asked his fiancée. "An intruder, right?"

"Right. Our security's in place for specific functions and the night watchmen were there to report something like that. The culprit could've been caught then and there."

"You'll have to take action," Kurt said to his daughter.

"I know and I intend to."

"What if the culprit wasn't there?" Gabrielle asked. Her chest felt hot and her palms sweaty. "At the Pearl that night. Would you fire the watchmen anyway?"

"Gabby...?" Kimberly's eyebrows rose and dropped. "Why the hypotheticals?"

"They—" she cleared her throat "—they're not hypotheticals. The culprit wasn't in the Pearl that night. I was there."

"Oh, you were? Then that's fine. Why didn't you say something sooner?"

"Because I wasn't alone." She glanced around the grand room that suddenly felt like a narrow tunnel. "I had a guest."

"So late?" Robyn asked at the same time that Kurt Parker asked, "Who was the guest?"

"Geoffrey Girard was with me. We were looking at things for the gala at the end of the month, and then I was making a chocolate sauce. Uh, the sauce burned and some pans fell off the counter. That's what alerted the watchmen to check in on things. One of them caught us..."

"Caught you looking at stuff for the gala and making sauce?" Kimberly blinked. "I don't see the big deal about that."

"Well," Gabrielle said, hesitating and rubbing her palms on her knees, "he caught us kissing and he noticed that we'd let the sauce burn while we were making out."

Robyn was leaning forward. "You said kissing. Then you said making out."

"Yeah, kissing half dressed." Gabrielle stood up. "I'm so sorry. It was a crazy thing to do, and I should've been using my brain. I know he and I shouldn't have been there alone so late. And we shouldn't have been making out on a counter and knocking things on the floor."

"Okay, now we're getting a clearer picture. A watchman got more than he bargained for on that shift, didn't he?"

Gabrielle nodded. "Kim, please don't fire those men. They didn't report anything because it was me and I'd asked him for discretion. I didn't want you and Robyn and everyone else to know what I'd done."

"Don't you mean with whom you were doing it?" her friend said levelly.

"Yes. I do mean that. I'm so sorry, Jaxon and Kimberly, for judging you the way I did when I first found out what might be developing between the two of you. Nobody asks for attraction that complicates things. I certainly didn't. I've been trying to resist what I feel for Geoffrey, but I can't do it."

"Why didn't you just tell us?" Robyn asked.

"Because I wanted to stick to my guns about the implied 'no fraternizing' rule. I didn't want to be a hypocrite."

Kimberly crossed her arms. She looked vulnerable for a quick second then was back to calm confidence. "You're the one forcing yourself to adhere to that, Gabby. You're the only one saying 'live this way' and then if *you* don't, you paint yourself into a corner you can't get out of."

"She said she's sorry and I'm accepting that she is," Jaxon said to Kimberly.

"I know she is, but look, Gabby, you're hurting yourself and this time you could've hurt those security guards by causing them to lose their jobs."

"I realize that. Again, I'm sorry."

Sometimes it was acceptable to play games in business, but never in relationships. Geoffrey wasn't out to deceive or be deceived. When he arrived a half hour early at the Pearl for his dinner with Gabrielle, he'd done it for two reasons.

One, he was eager to see her.

Two, he knew she'd get there early to have time to pop in on the kitchen, and he wanted to be there to remind her that there'd be a bit of role reversal at the Pearl tonight. She'd be a guest, not a chef. She wouldn't come to the table and discuss a wine list or prepare a menu or trot to the kitchen to cook.

Tonight she'd sit in the dining room and experience having someone else cater to her needs. She was so devoted to her career that he knew her beautiful was more natural than it was man-made. She appeared high-maintenance but turned out not to be. It was all her. Authentically her.

But things were supposed to be different for this dinner. He wanted to be with her in an environment that she knew, but at the same time he wanted to have her to himself.

"What can I get you this evening?" the old bartender Jonah asked in a voice that was in the middle between cheerful and crotchety. The selection behind him glimmered, their contents tempted.

Geoffrey tried to avoid linking his father's past with choices he could control for himself. There was no one hundred percent positivity that he'd become dependent on alcohol, as his father had been. There was no guarantee that he'd lose sight of what he valued, would destroy those he loved, in a vortex of addiction. Nevertheless, he said to the bartender, "No thanks, Jonah."

"You have a story, don't you, Mr. Girard?"

"Yeah." Geoffrey relaxed into a gruff chuckle. "I'd say you have about three times as many stories as I do."

"You know, that may be right. I've lived your life two, maybe three times, going by the look of you. That makes me a good listener, though. So give me something to listen to so I can feel useful."

Ironically, someone approached the bar requesting a complicated drink, and the elderly man fixed it with startling precision and style. He got applause and a healthy tip for his trouble.

"That blew her away," Geoffrey said, shaking Jonah's hand. "You did the damn thing."

"That's what I do. The damn thing." Jonah huffed a laugh. "Okay, so you've finagled a date with my favorite chef, have you? Oh, I have this way of knowing what happens around here—sometimes before it happens."

"Especially when you have a hand in making it happen, like when you got me to meet her to begin with."

"That's fair."

"It's a dinner."

"You mean a date?"

"We're not calling it that."

"Bull. It's a date. Now, then. Your first in-public, *appropriate location* date with her? No after-closing funny business this time?"

Geoffrey smoothed his suit lapels. That'd been Gabrielle's idea, but the technicalities weren't all that important. "Right, Jonah."

"Ah, okay. What do you like about her? Can't say she's a typical girl you catch sashaying here in Belleza or in Palm Springs and the like. Some of our own get swept away in the glamour California's supposed to be all about."

"You're not impressed by much, are you, Jonah."

"Too old. What's your excuse?"

"I've seen too much." Geoffrey didn't reject the glass of ginger ale the bartender set in front of him without being asked. "Bad stuff, a lot of it. It leaves scars that can't be fixed."

"I understand. What makes Gabby someone you want to take out? I'd say you were a very busy man and spend your time sagely."

"It's what you said. She's a different kind of woman. Natural, three-dimensional. Smart as a friggin' whip and compassionate, too."

"And you like the look of her?"

"Yeah. Can't get her out of my head."

"That, my friend, is one of the world's unexplained wonders. You've seen too much, you've got those un-fixable scars, but she's in your head anyway and you feel hopeful." Jonah smiled. "She's unique, that one. Strong-willed. A weak man won't do for her."

Geoffrey looked around the dining room. Talking about her made him ache to see her. "I'm the man for her. She's for me, too. She doesn't want my money. Know how many women have passed through my life just to dip their hands into my money? It'd be sad if it weren't so screwed up."

"Treasure," he thought the old man murmured.

"What was that?"

"Nothing. Well, I'm sure it's not just the money they want. Popularity?"

"Guess so. No choice of my own, but I was recently named one of LA's most eligible bachelors. It was the equivalent of putting a personal's ad on a billboard. It's made life a bit more hellish."

"Sorry to hear that. I can see how the ladies would be smitten with a man like you. You remind me of a reincarnation of James Bond. Anyone ever tell you that?"

Geoffrey frowned. "No. Can't say they have."

"Young people. Your imaginations are too limited. I blame those new phones everyone walks around with. If people got a chance to miss their electronics, they'd start to rely on their imaginations more. That's my theory, anyway."

"Sorry, but I can't test that theory for you. I need my phone."

"All right. Just don't stare at it while you're on a date with my gal."

"I can promise you that won't happen." When she was around, he found it tough to look at anything else.

"Good. Then all I can say is, if you're lucky enough to have Gabby's love, don't let it go. The thing is, you have to deserve it."

"We never said this was a date," Gabrielle told her friends as they gathered in her bedroom to help her get ready for the dinner she'd agreed to have with Geoffrey at the Pearl. "I swear, if I'm needed I will be cooking food in that kitchen before anyone can say boo."

"That's expected," Robyn said. "The Pearl is your baby. We understand that now, and Geoffrey probably does, too."

"Do you think I don't know *how* to date? Is that why this is so difficult for me?" she wondered.

"I think you were burned by watching how people moved in your family's world. Guys went after you to get in good with your parents and get connections. It burned you and that's not your fault. But, Gabby, Robyn and I aren't going to stand in your way of being happy with Geoffrey. If he's the one for you, we're just here to give you advice and stop you from derailing everything, if we can." Kimberly sat at Gabrielle's vanity, sniffing her assortment of perfumes.

"Ha." Gabrielle made a face, which Kimberly could see through the mirror.

"If you keep food off your dress and refrain from making that face over dinner, you're golden. All right. So, on this nondate, do you want your scent to say 'look, smell and want but don't touch' or 'touch, touch and touch'?"

Gabrielle considered her options as she shimmied into the strapless black cocktail dress her friends had helped her find at an exclusive eveningwear boutique the night before.

"Think it over," Kimberly said as the doorbell rang. "Finish getting ready and I'll answer the door. Is he picking you up here at the condo?"

"No, I'm supposed to meet him at the restaurant. But I want to get there early so I can pop in on the kitchen and see how everyone's doing."

"Don't you think they're going to be nervous enough to be preparing your food?" Robyn asked. "You're very particular."

"Perfection is what the Belleza wants."

"True."

Kimberly returned with an intimidating-sized male at her side. "You'll never guess what the wind blew your way. He's a stray, Gabby, but he's just so adorable."

"Don't anger the beast," Stu said, but he was grinning. He turned his clear blue eyes to Gabrielle. "Chef Royce, you look smashing."

"And look, he's bearing fruit," Robyn said, pointing to the large crate in his arms.

"Our supplier said you requested every citrus they could offer. Three samples of each. Chef Joon said the two of you will be working on the signature dessert here until it's time to bring the pastry team into the loop."

"That's right. Could you take that to the kitchen?"

"You really do look smashing."

"Chef Merritt, you said that already."

"I know. It's just that I'm accustomed to you in Pearl-wear and that grunge-chic look you're always rocking. Demure looks sexy on you."

"The last time you called me sexy, we were singing that The Mamas & the Papas song at that rundown pub in London. We were so awful that somebody paid us to stop singing, saying the building would collapse if we kept on."

Laughing, he carried the crate off and Kimberly called after him, "She's almost ready for her *non*date with the boss. Would you mind fixing her a nice mild drink, please? She's a little nervous, but she's covering it up pretty damn well." She winked at Gabrielle. "We've been friends way too long for you to fool me with your C plus acting skills."

Stu came back with a clear drink as Robyn asked, "Gabby, are you still packing that old condom you won at that adult-themed carnival we went to that time?"

"Yes."

"Somebody give her something. I don't think she's

ready for a baby just yet. Can you imagine, though? A dominant alpha dad plus a dominant and alpha mom would make one hell of an intense kid."

"Yo. I didn't say I was going to sleep with anyone. And who says *I'm* alpha."

Kimberly, Robyn and Stu all turned to stare slack-jawed at her.

"Okay, go home. All of you."

"Even me?" Stu asked, swallowing down the drink, since she'd dismissed him.

"Not you, smart aleck. I know you have a shift at the restaurant."

"You concentrate on staying out of the kitchen. Don't micromanage while you're on a date, woman."

Gabrielle finished getting ready quickly after they all cleared her condo. She blasted The Rolling Stones and took a moment to take inventory of the fruit that the restaurant's suppliers had sent over. She and Nicola Joon would need to set aside a day, at least, to experiment with the citrus offerings, but she had all the faith in the world that the signature dessert would be perfected in time to unveil at the Dunham Foundation's gala in September.

When she entered the Pearl, she was carried back to the past to the moment she'd first unofficially met Geoffrey. The memory shattered quickly because things were so much different now. He was just as scrumptious now as he had been the day he'd pushed open the kitchen doors and put her on the defensive, but now they knew each other and for the first time they weren't sneaking around.

As if he had radar on her, he lifted his head and

turned to her. A slow smile spread across his mouth but didn't quite reach his intense dark eyes.

She joined him at a table. A moment later Jonah set a glass of wine in front of her and said, "Compliments of the gentleman sitting across from you."

Geoffrey glanced at his watch. "Didn't expect you for another twenty minutes." His gaze casually cruised over her and the appreciative gleam in his eyes gave hope that her expensive designer dress was worth the splurge.

"I figured I'd get here a bit early to, ah, get my bearings."

"Or to check on your staff?"

"Maybe that, too."

He laughed, and looked too damned good. "You're full of surprises. I like that."

Gabrielle eyed him skeptically. Wow, he was being awfully candid and honest and *sweet*. The cynic in her wondered how he'd become quite so relaxed when usually there was silky yet unbreakable tension surrounding him. Was he that relieved that they didn't have to sneak around anymore? Or had he let tonight be a night for drinking? Before she could guess, his cell phone rang and he eased away from the table.

"I need to take this call," he told her. "Damage control. Order what you want and I'll be back in a bit."

As he strode away, she surrendered to the naughty urge to stare at his ass. Great butt, magnificent abs, sexy face and hands that knew how to control her like a marionette. If the combo belonged to anyone but a Belleza guest, she'd have had the thrill of her life by now.

The atmosphere around her was elegant yet comfortable. People were seated at the beautifully set tables, and soft music wafted down from the intercoms. Glancing around for Geoffrey, she murmured, "Oh, what the hell?" and got up.

In the kitchen, one of the line cooks said, "She's here! It's under fifteen minutes. Give me my money."

"What? Y'all were betting how long it'd be before I came into the kitchen?" she asked.

The kitchen erupted in laughter, and though she was the ass of the joke, she didn't mind all that much. They all knew her, and she knew them. It made her feel sorry to even attempt to suspect any of them of trying to sabotage the Belleza.

How could any of these people be responsible for intentionally harming one of their own?

The doors opened and Stu came in. "Chef Royce, you should know that instead of babysitting us, you should be worrying about your date. Hostess Hottie just brought a bottle of bubbly to your table and is taking the liberty of having a glass with him."

Charlene? What was the woman thinking? Maybe Jonah had been right about her when he'd called her aggressive.

"Thanks for keeping Geoffrey company while I checked on things, Charlene," Gabrielle said brightly, not wanting to come off as a wild-eyed lioness defending what was hers.

Charlene fluffed her golden curls. "He said you two were on a date and, forgive me, I didn't right off find that true, because… I mean… My mistake, Gabs."

"Char? Popping up in front of this man every time my back is turned, that's not cool. I'm asking you once to stop."

"Fine." The woman's eyes snapped envy for a moment, but as she stood, she said, "We should hang out in LA sometime. I told Geoffrey that my friends and I have a singing gig at a club. You should come. Bring him."

"I'll think about it. Thanks."

"Have a good time." Charlene bounced off, sneering at the bartender on her way to the hostess desk.

Geoffrey waited for Gabrielle to take her seat before he said, "Saw what she did there?"

"You mean how she was blatantly making a move on you then she got a stank attitude with me then she acted like we're friends who can just go to LA clubs and hang out?"

"Not *any* club."

"The one where she and her friends sing. And she suggested that I bring you." That wasn't quite aggression or ambition. It was aggressive ambition. "Do you want to go someplace else?"

"As tempting as it sounds to get you someplace where you won't be running to the kitchen to check on things, I'm good with staying here. It reminds me of that first day, when you hesitated before you even sat down and tasted the sauvignon blanc."

"When I offered the wine, I didn't know about your issues with alcohol."

"I'm thinking tonight I can ease up on those issues. You enjoy wine and I'm going to share that with you."

"I wouldn't ask you to do that for me."

"I'm offering. It's my hang-up and it doesn't control me."

Gabrielle watched him order bourbon and she ordered the same. She appreciated alcohol, but didn't know how he'd fare, being a lightweight. It'd be too easy to overestimate what he could handle. And the fact that he was starting in heavy before they'd even begun eating rang all sorts of warning bells.

When they ordered their meals, he still seemed sober. But by the time the food had arrived, he was on his third bourbon and she was wondering if they'd end the night with her calling him a cab or waiting embarrassed at the table while he got sick in the restroom. Imagine *that* publicity.

Haunted Resort's Chef Gets Music God Wasted.

"Waiter, another bourbon, please," he requested in a tone that sounded more like a heated demand. His eyes landed on her. "You're not drinking. Why not?"

Because we can't both *be shit-faced drunk.* "I'm not very thirsty," she replied. The waiter approached with a carafe of coffee and a mug. At least she wasn't worried about Geoffrey's blood alcohol level. "But you obviously are."

"I'm not thirsty. I think I had too much," he said openly.

"That's why Jonah brought coffee."

"Jonah. Nice old guy. Slick as hell. He set us up. My order. He took the order and made it so we'd meet."

Gabrielle turned toward the bar, where Jonah Grady was too slow to play off that he was watching them. So nice old guy was Cupid in disguise. She never in her kookiest dreams would have guessed.

"How do you feel about being manipulated that way?" she asked.

"Thankful."

She had dealt with a few drunk friends and some even drunker strangers in her time, but none had been so open and honest.

"We never talked about your family," he said.

"I'm not doing this." Chin up, mouth firm and eyes level to silently say "I mean business," Gabrielle tried not to think about the people in her past who wanted part of her present and were only interested in controlling her future.

But persistence, charm and intimidation made Geoffrey someone virtually impossible to say no to.

She could attest to that. How else had she gone from being irked by him to wanting to slip her underwear into his pocket? She didn't know him, and yet he could turn her on like a switch.

When she had realized that others had sought her out not because they wanted to see her but because they wanted to pump her for information about her family instead, she'd told them flat-out to hitchhike to hell and then locked herself in her house. Now, seeing that Geoffrey refused to be brushed off and didn't seem to be interested in personal gain, she wasn't with very many options.

"Why do you want to know?"

"I want to know because I'd like to know you better. I'm asking you because I didn't look you up on Google to take a shortcut into your life. You seem to agree that a little research is sometimes required to get the job done." He lifted a shoulder in a lazy half shrug and settled his eyes on hers.

"Oh."

No elaboration followed.

Since he didn't seem particularly concerned with her current career options, she said, "So what does this dinner have to do with where I come from? I feel as though you're flirting with me. But are you deceiving me instead?"

It didn't seem possible, but she'd swear she saw his eyes darken further. "I don't have an angle with you."

A shadowed, reluctant corner inside her wasn't convinced, but she nodded.

"There's not much to talk about. I told you about my grandmother May and how she gave me the money to pursue cooking school. And there are other people, my parents and brothers, but they didn't exactly support my career path. We don't have to get bogged down with those details." At any rate, he'd wake up in the morning feeling as if there was a party going on in his head and wouldn't remember what they talked about tonight.

"You're holding something back," he accused, his brows furrowing. "It's all right, though. More for me to discover myself. I want to get to know you bits at a time." He suddenly stood. "I want to get outta here. Can't take my car. I need a ride." He swayed and she leaped up to steady him. His hand splayed against her waist and his face lowered. "Oh, you smell really good. You smell like an invitation."

She blinked. "An invitation for what?"

"Sex."

Her blood flowed with arousal. For an instant she wanted to meet his lips, but she opted not to. "Why don't you spend the night here at the Belleza? Sit here—don't have any more drinks—and I'll get you a room."

He didn't resist, but trusted her to discreetly set him up in a room. He handed her his keys and left a tip on the table before they left the restaurant. In the parking lot, he was starting to droop beside her. She braced an arm around his middle and tugged him along. "In you go," she said, assisting him into his car with less finesse than she'd hoped. She thought she heard his head bang against the roof on the way in, and stopped to check him out. "You okay?" she asked, hopping in and turning the key in the ignition.

"Yeah."

She let him crank up the radio as she drove to the cottage she'd pulled strings to rent for him. When she ushered him inside, she said, triumphantly, "Home."

"Wait, this isn't home."

"It is for tonight."

"The date. I made a disaster of it."

"Are we calling it a date?"

"Jonah said it's a date."

"Geoffrey, I get what you were trying to do. You were trying to share my relationship with alcohol. It doesn't affect every person the same. We can't tolerate it the same way. But I don't want you to think you have to change yourself for me. That wouldn't be fair to you or to me."

"You're not pissed?"

"No. You're kind of sweet when you're like this, but I prefer you sober and intense. I prefer you as you are. So if you don't want to drink, don't." She touched his face. "Your head is going to ache so much tomorrow."

"It's already starting. Did we bring any of that coffee?"

"Uh-uh, but I'll fix some before I leave."

He was already walking toward the bedroom, already undressing. "Can you stay?"

"No, I can't." She went to the bedroom, peeled back a corner of the soft comforter and fluffed the pillows.

The gigantic four-poster bed looked so inviting that she would've liked to tumble onto it. *With him.*

"You deserve a perfect date. I'm going to give you that one day."

"Worry about getting some rest and coffee. I'll see you in the morning."

Her back was to him but she heard him shuffle across the room toward her. Then she felt his hands lightly caress the length of her bare back and knew that they were both beckoning disaster. He interlaced his fingers with hers and brought her hand to his lips. "I'm drunk, right? I've never been drunk before."

"I first got drunk at a party when I was nineteen. I woke up in somebody's closet with a soccer ball under my head. I found out what my limit was and I never go past that. I get close and I get loose, but it's important to stay in control."

"Tell me about it."

"We'll talk about it another time," she told him, and steered him to the bed. "Call me if you need anything." As he fell asleep, she lowered to the bed and threaded her fingers through his hair.

Feeling like a child giving up a piece of coveted candy, she rose and quietly left his house.

Chapter 9

When Kimberly and Robyn had noticed Gabrielle was home—alone—early from her date, she told them that something had come up for Geoffrey and she had work to do anyway if the signature dessert was going to be perfected in time for the Dunham Foundation gala. Satisfied with that, they'd left her alone.

She got up early the next morning to squeeze in a hot yoga session with the ladies at the Belleza's gym, then she showered and arrived at Geoffrey's emergency cottage armed with a thermos filled with steaming coffee and a plate of blueberry muffins.

Geoffrey greeted her at the door clad only in the pants he'd worn to dinner last night. His face was unshaven, and his eyes weary. The angry set of his mouth softened into a surprised smile when he saw her. "Gabrielle…what are you doing here?"

"I said I'd check on you, but I'm not surprised that

you don't remember. Your car is here. I had the resort valet drive me back to get mine."

"Thing is, I remember everything. I wish I hadn't overdone it on the bourbon." He pushed the door open wider and paused to give her an approving once-over. Today she wore a gray rayon sundress and matching sweater. On her feet were dressy sandals. "Is that outfit new?"

"Nope, but I've been a lazy girl in the laundry department, so I'm low on pieces to complete my 'grunge-chic' look."

"You're…"

"What?" she challenged.

Not backing down, he snared her gaze. "Sexy. You look completely sexy. C'mon in."

Floating on a cloud of flattery, she followed him inside and enjoyed the view of his bare back. What a wonderful, muscular back. If she was a cartoon, her tongue would be rolling out onto the floor right now. "Uh, I brought you breakfast. Nothing spectacular, just muffins and coffee. I imagine you really just want the coffee."

"Thankfully I don't have a killer hangover."

"Are you planning to go back to the Hills right away?"

"Around noon. My assistant and I need to get in contact with a few publicists. There's something happening at the company. Somebody's trying to poach on our talent."

When they arrived in the living room, he turned to accept the food. "Sorry about last night. What you said was spot-on. It doesn't help either of us to force a change. Go ahead and have a seat on the couch and I'll grab some dishes."

She took the opportunity to look around. The cottage had large rooms and plenty of windows. Even a sunroom. The living room was in slight disarray. She could tell from the bottle of aspirin and his phone on the table that he'd been busy with work before she arrived.

The guy didn't even slow down to adequately sleep off a hangover.

She walked through the spacious, sunny living room to an even sunnier kitchen. There were top-of-the-line appliances, and attractive stainless steel sinks and faucets complemented the cream-colored walls and slate-colored marble topped counters. But the beauty of the room was secondary to the yummy man standing at the counter arranging the muffins on a plate. "Need a hand?" she offered.

"You've done enough," he told her. "Thanks for dealing with me."

"You weren't too tough to deal with. You were actually very sweet."

"You were sexy and someone I was thankful for."

She wondered if he'd backpedal on what he'd said to her last night. But here he was, sober, and still sticking to his story. She watched him suddenly hesitate as if debating, then he crossed the room to her, slid his hands lightly up her arms to frame her face in his hands.

"What are you doing?"

The streaming sunshine glowed over the sharp contours of his face. His mouth curved into a frown and his eyes fiercely searched hers. "Do I need to answer that in words?"

His head moved toward hers.

A shiver rocked through her as his hands moved up the sides of her face and his thumb rubbed over her lips.

Gabrielle splayed her fingers through his hair. With his chest rising and falling so close to her, she felt his warmth. Then his lips landed on her throat.

"Gabrielle…"

"I think now it's okay for you to call me Gabby."

In response, she tilted her face upward a fraction and sighed to take the kiss. His mouth softly tested hers. Then he deepened the kiss as his tongue coaxed her lips open farther to touch her tongue. The electricity of the intimate encounter washed away any remnants of his hesitation.

When he dropped back, she felt disoriented and on fire. Her arms encircled his waist and his shallow, uneven breath whistled in her hair. "What'd I do to deserve kisses?"

His arms looped around her waist and his hands cupped her shoulder blades to draw her even closer. "You could've let me make a complete ass of myself at the Pearl, but you didn't. You're a good person." He rubbed his lips over hers before peppering soft, sweet kisses over her closed eyelids then to her temple, and then releasing her. "Thanks."

Dazed with lust, Gabrielle barely nodded. She hadn't come here expecting this, but now that he seemed to be done arousing her silly, she felt deprived and let down. Inhaling deeply, she hoped that a few cleansing breaths would cool the fire kindling at the apex of her thighs.

"Who's manning the restaurant now?"

"Competent people. Just because I tend to micromanage things doesn't mean I don't trust my staff. I'm not turning any of them into management and accusing them of trying to make our company implode."

"Where'd that come from?"

"That's the newest development. Management's concerned that an insider is behind the strange occurrences. Um, this isn't making the Belleza less appealing for Phenom Jones's party, is it?"

"G&G Records has a way of surviving trials like that. It's going to survive underhanded bastards trying to steal our talent, too."

"I'm sorry that's happening."

"It's part of the business. Not a part I like, but…" He rolled his shoulders. "Now, to talk about something I *do* like. You can handle anything. You amaze me."

"Keep talking. I've got time."

"If I stopped talking, would you stay here? Because I'm thinking about doing something and you might shut me down."

"Or I might not." She probably should leave, weigh her options, factor in her skyrocketing horniness, maybe do something productive such as work while she thought this over. But, he was so mouth-watering in those pants. And besides, why not share a little appetizer of what she was capable of? "You didn't get to make an empire of G&G by shying away from risks. Take the risk now. Am I worth it to you?"

"Hell, yes." And he had her mouth.

He didn't linger there, though. Quickly, he tasted her throat, filled his hands with her breasts, demanded that she not hold back what she felt. If she didn't like something, he wanted to know. If she did like something, he *needed* to know.

When his hand brushed her breast again, she watched him as she gasped. And then he gripped the front of her sweater and ripped it open, sending the delicate pearl buttons skittering across the floor.

"Yeah, this is one of the few sweaters I hadn't destroyed. Before now."

"I can replace it for you."

"No, it's cool. I'll make a necklace with the buttons and I'm sure there's something I can do to jazz up the fabric. Maybe shorten— Oh…my…"

He'd bunched the bottom of her dress in his fists and was shooting it up over her head. He stared at her breasts swelling modestly over the cups of her lightning bolt–patterned bra. "Party underneath, right."

"Uh-huh."

"The party's underneath this," he said, hooking a finger under a bra strap. He clamped it in his teeth and pulled it down.

Arousal shot through her when he hauled her against the island. She felt his hand snake up her thigh beneath the hemline of her dress and cup her there.

"I've been wanting to get back at this since that night in the car." He tugged her panties down, let her kick them away. As he slid two fingers inside her, his mouth found the tips of her breasts. He nipped her flesh through the bra before he quit playing and impatiently unhooked the garment. It bounced off her lap and hit the floor and there was nothing interfering with his access to her bare skin.

She cried out a zing of pleasure, kneaded his shoulders even if he didn't need to be guided. What his fingers didn't touch, his teeth did, and soon she was leaning weakly against the counter for support. She scooted onto a stool.

"Let me help you out," he said, then picked her up.

She felt herself moisten more. Then the cool surface of the island touched her ass. "Yow! That's cold."

"It won't be after a minute."

"Yeah? Well, you take off your pants and sit up here and tell me how it feels."

"Trust me."

She began to scoff, but he reached behind her and knocked away the coffee and muffins. Her gasp drowned out the sound of shattering dishes when he firmly ran his hands over her breasts. He urged her to lie back, flat on the counter. He spread her thighs. "Sorry about the muffins."

"I can bake more," she said, swallowing. "I just don't want them to become props in what we're doing here. I don't use food for sex play."

"Not whipped cream?"

"No food."

"Think about opening yourself to the idea of it."

He pushed her thighs apart wider and licked her. She arched up and let loose a scream that only seemed to encourage him to keep going. She was no longer "Sorry, I'm closed" for this guest. The invisible bear trap didn't exist. She wasn't an executive chef and he a big-shot music producer client. She was a naked woman and he was an almost naked man.

She would make things fair and get him out of those pants *after* she finished losing wits completely at the demands of his tongue.

His hand snaked up her abdomen to seize her breasts. As he rolled and pinched her nipples, his mouth continued to tantalize her. He slipped two fingers inside her, pulled them out and then repeated the motion and his tongue glided over her clit. He closed his lips over the sensitive bead and caressed her firmly with the very tip of his tongue.

She sobbed restlessly on the island, her legs spread wide and her eyes squeezed shut. When she dared to open them, to watch him taste her, he lifted his eyes to hers and smiled against her flesh before the orgasm struck.

There was good sex, unbelievable sex and the kind of sex that melted a sensible man's mind. Geoffrey didn't have a mind to rely on now. He could lead this woman and make moves on her body, but he wasn't in control. And he didn't mind. He was so turned on to see her come in his mouth. Leaning over her, he trailed kisses up her rib cage, to her nipples that were borderline burgundy from his hands and teeth. Her mouth was parted and ready for his when he reached her, and he slipped his tongue inside.

He fed her a sample of herself, let her lick into his mouth and tease his tongue to dance with hers. Their bodies were hot and sweat-dampened, and her hips were still twitching from her orgasm. He murmured into her mouth, "Want to keep at it?"

"Damn, skippy. We are not done. You owe me some nakedness, for one thing."

She moaned and he knew he had to have her. Any way, every way. Now.

The need was real and yet intangible. His cock throbbed against his zipper, pleading for her. He slapped at his pockets. Nothing. No condom!

"You're not going to believe this."

"You don't have protection?"

"No."

"So for our date you weren't *expecting* sex?"

"No. I didn't know if you'd be ready and wasn't going to rush you if you weren't."

She sat up and hugged him. "You're not an asshole. You're sweet."

"The other word that starts with the letter *A*. It was *asshole*?"

"Uh…yup. What'd you think it was?"

"Adventurous. Accomplished. Articulate. Awesome. Something along those lines."

"You're going to be telling me *I'm* awesome when I tell you that I have a condom. I do. It's in my purse."

He kissed her. "You are so awesome." He brought the purse to her and she fished out the condom and gave it to him. "Gabrielle, this has a Ferris wheel on it."

"Yeah, I got it at this adult-themed carnival." She began laughing and didn't stop until he'd whisked her up and brought her to the bedroom. She felt good in his arms, all naked and sweaty and ready for the main course. When he deposited her onto the unmade bed, she pulled him to her.

She leisurely slid over his body, arching like a cat, and fastened her hands on his zipper. She lowered the zipper and pulled his pants over his hips, freeing him. "Ohh," she sighed, her gaze washing over his penis and giving him the same effect as if she'd just used her mouth on him. When she bent to do just that, he hurriedly took her face in his hands.

"If I let you do this, I won't last long enough to get

inside you." Then he proved that by swiftly sheathing himself, spreading her thighs and thrusting inside her. She was so slick and so incredibly tight his mind went momentarily numb.

"Are you a virgin?"

Her head twisted from side to side and she said, "I know some people who'd laugh you out of town at that question. I redeemed my V-card years ago, but it's been a while. So long, in fact, that my friends and colleagues were pushing me to get out there and meet someone. Turns I didn't have to go anywhere. You came to me." She stroked his arm. "I'm glad you came to me."

He gazed at the tousled, glistening woman underneath him, loving how the morning sunlight washed over her skin. She pressed a gentle hand to the side of his face and he covered it with his.

Their gazes locked and he watched her brown eyes widen and her lips part as her muscles stretched to adapt to him. But he knew how to lean against her and thrust slowly to give her pressure and pleasure. He held her shaking body and brought them to a slamming climax.

"Where the hiz-ell have you been?" Charlene asked when Gabrielle passed the hostess desk around noon.

Damn!

Busted.

After a catnap in an erotic position with Geoffrey, Gabrielle had reluctantly dragged her worn-out and somewhat sore self into what was left of her clothes and went home to dress for work. With Jimi Hendrix in the background, she'd showered, pulled on dressy black capri pants and a frilly white blouse. She'd embroidered the words *The Pearl* onto it and it was one of her favorites. In a hurry to get to the restaurant at least before noontime, she'd piled her messy hair up high and rubbed on eye shadow and lipstick. But standing here under the hostess's scrutiny, she felt swamped in self-consciousness and imagined the words *just had sex* branded on her forehead.

Noticing a few curious glances of guests as Charlene followed Gabrielle into the kitchen, she said, "Is there a problem? I'm not late, if we're being technical."

"There *is* a problem. Some dude's been asking a lot of questions and making everyone nervous. He grilled Jonah Grady so harshly that I felt sorry for him. What do you know about this?"

"We're all aware there have been strange incidents around the resort lately. Management is out to protect everyone and I'm sure some questioning is necessary."

"Questioning would be fine if it were from the police," Stu said. "This bloke wasn't the police."

Kim's PI. That made sense. "Did he leave any contact information with y'all?"

The kitchen staff all murmured no and returned to their work, but the tension was thick enough to suffocate someone.

"Where were you this morning?" Charlene pressed, eyes narrowed. Did the woman have a sex tracking device or something?

"Not here."

"You should've been."

"Enough, Charlene," one of the cooks said. "Go back to your desk and do your job, instead of making sure other people are doing theirs."

Huffing, the hostess fled the kitchen. Gabrielle covered her hair and washed up at the sink. "I can speak to management and find out if there's any development, but no one here has anything to worry about."

"You might not," someone grumbled. "You can sneak around with guests after hours and you still have the top job at this restaurant. Management's looking to fire people, and you're secure but we're not."

"Our management is fair. When those reviews about bad food and all that crap fell down on us, I took the heat. Management has protocol and follows it. It wasn't smart for me to invite a guest into this kitchen after closing, but it's not as though he was here alone and for that matter I work in this kitchen after hours all the time. It's not a precedent I set. It's not that unusual."

Under the circumstances, she should've been more prudent. She hadn't been, and now she was paying the price. The cost was her staff's respect and trust. These individuals looked up to her even as she considered them equals. Her friendship with Kimberly Parker may not have mattered to them before, but it did now in the wake of her showing up to the restaurant after every Pearl employee but she had been "grilled." They suspected that she'd known about the ambush and had stayed away on purpose. She hadn't known, but how could she tell them the truth about where she'd been and what she'd been doing without making the situation that much worse?

Sorry I wasn't here to be questioned with the rest of you. I was getting power-tooled by one of the Belleza's most high-profile guests—you know, Geoffrey Girard, the man I sneaked into the kitchen and made out with that night?

"Can't tell them that," she whispered to herself. Of course she'd try to be more diplomatic, but that's how it'd translate to them. It wouldn't sound pretty or gentle or like anything they were obligated to forgive.

She'd screwed up in a big way and was far away from making amends.

At the same time, she thought, as she kicked into high gear and began to prepare a vegetable risotto for a multicourse meal, these were the same people who not even a month ago had been urging her to get into a relationship, or simply get laid. Now that she had, they weren't even happy for her?

"Is he a good guy?"

Gabrielle looked beside her at Stu. "Why ask? Would it make a difference? The general consensus is that I'm the chef who selfishly sent her staff up the river because I'm friends with management."

"Petulance is unattractive on you. You know I'm not mad at you, and you're incapable of being mad at me because I'm effing incredible, so just answer the question already. Oh, what is this, risotto?"

"Yes, it's risotto. I answered your question."

"What'd I just tell you about petulance?"

"Chef Merritt, he's a good guy. He can't handle booze, but I don't mind at all." She noticed Stu moving his hand as if turning a wheel. "Oh, you big dirty chef. You only want to know about the sex."

"Was there?" he whispered, though no one was close by to hear.

"This morning. That's what I was doing while you all were being hassled. I feel bad about it."

"Bad about what? What was the quality of the sex?"

"Top quality. My God." She shook her head. "I feel

bad that I wasn't here with all of you. We're in this together. That's what it means to be a team."

"They'll get over it. They're worried about being
the next victim more than they're worried about being
fired. No one wants to say they're scared shitless. As
someone who was a victim not long ago, I can tell
you it makes you watch yourself more carefully." He
tugged at her collar. "You have a hickey, Chef Royce."

Oops. "I do?"

"Yes." He hugged her. "I'm so proud."

After finishing the risotto, Gabrielle was drawn
away for office work and meetings that kept her occu-
pied for the next few hours. She ate a light lunch and
then was able to catch up with Kim.

"Is this about wedding details?" Kim asked as they
sat on a sleek bench outside one of the resort shops. In
a pantsuit the color of cool metal, and her hair hanging neatly past her shoulders, she was serenity and
style and unflappable power personified. "I thought
we'd coordinate our schedules and make a day of it."

Gabrielle only wished the wedding was all they
had to worry about. It was a tumultuous time to plan
such an event, but why wait when love was there?
"This is about a man who made rounds at the Pearl
today, apparently grilling all the staff, including
Jonah Grady. You know what it feels like to face
that many pissed off people all expertly trained in
wielding knives?"

"Are you thinking it was the investigator I hired?"

"Well, it wasn't Annie the Clairvoyant."

Kim knit her beautifully shaped eyebrows. "He reported to me that there were no clear connections, all

but insisted that this is all a string of coincidences. Maybe he found a reason to double back."

"Could you please get to the bottom of it, and find out why he's not keeping you informed ahead of the game? You're the one who hired him. He has no right to harass our staff on his own accord."

"But keep this straight, Gabby, I *did* hire him to do a job. If he has a lead and perhaps didn't have the time to clear his next move with me, I'm not going to be upset if it reveals new information about whoever's terrorizing this resort. I don't want to anger our employees any more than you do, but the fact still remains that something strange is happening and it's becoming increasingly more dangerous for not only the staff, but the guests. It's criminal activity. Are we agreed on that?"

"Certainly. There should be a better way, though."

"I'm sorry." She sat back against the bench. "Love is never easy."

"What, your road to romance with Jaxon?"

"Mmm, that and my love for the Belleza. I have a position that my brother thinks I stole out from under him. That didn't stop me from fighting like raging hell to catapult this place to the sort of success it never had before. The problems we faced last month and what's happening now—it's not going to break me. Am I alone in that belief?"

Gabrielle had always admired Kim's strength and wisdom. "You're not alone because you rubbed off on me. A big reason why I had the fortitude to strike out on my own after graduation is because I wanted to be more like you. So unafraid and tough."

"Say what? *You're* unafraid. Last Halloween you

toured that old vacant asylum and Robyn and I thought you were crazy. You do things like that all the time. You have a lust for life and good food and you do the weirdest shit to your clothes."

"Aw, you say the sweetest things, Kim." She took a deep breath and sat back, too. "About how I was when you were first interested in Jaxon. I'm sorry."

"You apologized for that."

"That was before I fully understood. I understand now. Love is far from easy and I made it worse by not supporting you. I get it now, Kim. I know what it means to be made to feel ashamed of something as miraculous as love."

"You're vouching for miracles, Gabby?"

"Absolutely. I've always believed in miracles. When I was in Spain I witnessed a woman give birth. I definitely believe in miracles. But I don't believe in the curse of the Belleza. And there were times when I didn't believe in love."

"And now?"

At first, all Gabrielle could do was nod. "Good grief, do I believe in love now."

When Gabrielle returned to the Pearl, there was a letter of resignation waiting on the hostess desk.

Charlene handed Gabrielle the letter, her face sapped of its usual sparkle. "This is a copy. The original has already been delivered to HR."

"You're quitting?"

The hostess squinted, drummed her acrylic nails on the desktop. "Me? No. Things are just getting juicy around here. Why would I miss out on the excitement?" She shook her shiny blond curls. "It's your assistant.

Roarke. He asked me to make sure you got this, and he took the original up to HR."

"Roarke? I was in the office with him earlier." They'd chatted about the resort's upcoming events and looked at silly YouTube videos and things had almost seemed normal between them.

"I know. Weird, isn't it? He took his stuff and walked out while you were gone. I heard a couple of the waitresses suggesting that he quit because of that man who came here asking questions. If Roarke had nothing to hide, why'd he go off the deep end and walk out on the company?"

"This makes no sense at all. That's not like him."

"Who's acting like themselves anymore anyway? One of the bussers said you wouldn't have sneaked a man into the restaurant for some rocking on the clock, but…" She shrugged. "And Jonah's been so wound up these past few days that he hasn't been able to perform any of those bartending tricks the guests love so much."

"I didn't rock on the clock."

"That's not what I heard. Or was it rocking in the dark?"

Gabrielle thanked the hostess for the note and felt a headache starting. Sometimes she had decent enough intentions, but her execution could use some work.

Sidling up to the bar, Gabrielle said, "Jonah, how about you take a seat. Take a break. Let's talk about stuff that has absolutely no importance."

Jonah's wrinkled face pulled into a grimace. "I saw you at the hostess desk, and now you're over here telling me to sit down. No, Gabby, I won't do that."

"I'm your friend. There's no cause for you to be so prickly, okay?"

"There's not? Strangers coming around, bringing the wrong sort of attention. The intrusive questions made every one of us feel like a wrongdoer, and that right there is a crime."

"That's fair to say, and I agree with you on that. But answer this completely honestly and I'll leave you alone. Are you not offering our bartending tricks for the guests because you don't want to, or because you can't?"

The regret in his eyes caused her physical pain.

"Oh, Jonah." She almost reached to pat his hand but knew he wouldn't appreciate the pity. "Take a break. Please. You're going to worry me. You're my friend and you're so rattled by this that you can't do what you love."

In response, the man stubbornly strode away to tend to an elegantly dressed couple interested in his recommendation.

Wounded, Gabrielle stood frozen there, watching him. She pleaded with her eyes because she couldn't speak through the concern and anguish.

Jonah, I can't lose you, too.

First her sous-chef, then her assistant. She wouldn't let her favorite bartender be next.

Jonah looked her way only once and when he turned his back to her, only then did she leave.

A few determined phone calls gave her only bits of information regarding her assistant's resignation. He definitely was gone, and he'd applied for employment at the Pinnacle, the Belleza Resort and Spa's direct competition. It wasn't until much later that Kim called her up to her office and shared that the man insisted he wasn't connected to the problems their company was facing and he'd cited that the reason he could no longer work for the Parkers was Gabrielle.

"He said he couldn't be your wingman anymore and watch you fall in love with someone else. Gabby, he has feelings for you. Did you know?"

Gabrielle felt like something she'd found on the bottom of her shoe once. She'd disposed of the shoe—both, actually—but couldn't so easily part with the havoc this bit of truth stirred.

Geoffrey had not only been right about Roarke's crush on her, but it'd been so intense that he felt he could no longer work with her. He'd rather work for the Belleza's new rival.

Bizarre didn't come close to describing this.

After work, Gabrielle called Geoffrey. When she told him that she'd lost another colleague, he was sympathetic. He suggested they go out to LA for dinner, but she had another idea and when she told him, he held her with total understanding in his eyes and in his touch.

"We went heavy on the TWIX, didn't we?" she asked him as they entered the lobby of the Belleza Medical Center. "And the Snickers?"

"Yeah. I can't believe she doesn't like KitKats, though." Geoffrey gravely shook his head at her. "Are you sure we're going to get along?"

"She'll adore you. She feels partly responsible for us getting together." They entered an elevator and she selected the floor where Shoshanna was staying. "Hours before I met you, she'd challenged me to hook up with the next sexy eligible man I met."

"Well, there are two ways I can interpret that. One is to feel flattered that you think I'm sexy. Another is to be unnerved that you might've picked another man."

"Be flattered. It took a while before I made up my mind about you, though."

"You were hard to get."

"You waited for me. Thanks for that." She tugged his sleeve as the doors opened. "She's self-conscious about her scars, but I think the candy will distract her."

They came into the room and Gabrielle said, "Shoshanna, I brought a man. And he's got candy." She beamed at Geoffrey. "Geoffrey Girard, meet Shoshanna Smirnov."

Shoshanna made grabby hands for the candy. "I like you already, Geoffrey. Really, it is a pleasure to meet the man who inspired Gabby to retire the bear trap between her legs."

They laughed and it felt more than right to incorporate him into her world. Robyn was half-smitten with him and Kimberly enamored. He could easily fit in her life, be the missing piece that she'd spent so many years ignoring.

She didn't believe in curses, but she had faith and trusted miracles and realized that love was possible for her. She *was* in love. It was fast and had developed so oddly, but fairy tale romances were for princesses and she was a free-spirited chef—a dandelion swaying in the wind.

Traditional, sensible love wasn't for her. Sudden, caught off guard love was.

She could see herself dancing with him at Kimberly's wedding. She could, in a very abstract visual, see him in her future. The two of them, together, committed, moving toward a happy ending, even.

Swiping a mini Snickers bar, she kissed his jaw and joined in the conversation.

Chapter 10

The eve of the G&G Records gala came fast. As it slid closer, Gabrielle found herself busier than usual. On top of helping Kimberly settle on the details for what was guaranteed to be a marvelous wedding, and training temporary staff for the Pearl, she and Nicola Joon had spent a total of forty-two hours tweaking the recipe for the signature dessert the Pearl would introduce in September. The condo smelled like citrus and though she wasn't altogether turned off by it, she was finding herself sick of finding ways to get rid of the leftover fruit the Pearl's produce supplier had given her.

Robyn had come over and crafted a gorgeously sophisticated fruit basket, which they'd all but forced Kimberly to give to her fiancé the next time she met up with him. Gabrielle was sick of making smoothies and sorbets, and as she stood in her kitchen cleaning to try and get her mind off the whirlwind tomorrow's massive event was guaranteed to be, she counted two oranges and a grapefruit remaining in the crate. Extracting the fruit, she put the crate away.

"What am I going to do with these things? Juggle them?" she asked herself, spying the fruit now on the counter. Before she allowed herself to be silly enough to try, she went to her bedroom closet and took out the outfit she'd bought for the gala. So many of the women would be in gowns and cocktail dresses, but Gabrielle would wear what represented her. The shimmery leggings and gilded off-the-shoulder sweater finished with gold high heels and her boldest wristwatch and bracelets would be sensational and she couldn't wait to see the full effect.

She wanted the night to be a success for Geoffrey and for it to be untainted with the sordidness of the resort's recent hell. Though she didn't dare mention it to her friends, she was nervous about the potential for disaster.

Even in a security-controlled environment, problems could arise.

She'd do whatever she could to protect her man. He'd changed her life, helped her discover real love and deserved to know she was thankful for him, too.

Pulse kicking up, Gabrielle put away the clothes and emerged from the walk-in closet to look at her bed. There was so much preparation to be done, but she knew *exactly* what she wanted to do for him tonight.

Geoffrey was close to cracking with tension. A rival record label had poached his newest client, a self-entitled diva blessed with a songbird voice and stage presence that had superstar written all over it, and based on this afternoon's conversation with his legal group that specialized in corporate and entertainment law, they were headed for court.

It was the same damned story. Put money in front of someone to find out their true colors. Fortune drove honest people to lie and triggered hatred among friends. Some said becoming a self-made man and rising to the top in the music industry had given him a thick skin, but to him it was a steel shield. It protected him but wouldn't allow the good things to truly reach him.

Alone in his office, designed by an internationally acclaimed architect, he was at the top of a Beverly Hills tower with the nighttime sky spread out for him. It was all glitter and darkness and meant nothing to him. His mind was stuck on lies and corporate deceit.

Of the guests who would be gathered poolside at the Belleza tomorrow evening in celebration of his empire's newly platinum artist, which had knives at the ready to sink into his back?

A timid knock on the door had him turning his back to the windows.

"Mr. Girard, your phone's off." Cathy, his lead office manager, was understated beauty in her calm gray pantsuit and the diamond broach he'd gifted her on her fifth-year anniversary with his company. Her voice was absent of accusation but rife with alarm.

"I thought I'd take a break." He swore and laughed, but nothing was funny and Cathy knew that. "I'll turn it back on."

"A call's come through. Gabrielle Royce is holding. Shall I tell her you're unavailable this evening?"

Unavailable to the one woman in his life he trusted above all others? "No, I'll pick up. It's getting late, Cathy. You go home."

"It doesn't seem fair, sir, that outside this office is a world that thinks you can want for absolutely nothing. Yet you're starving for the one thing humans need to survive in society."

"You can't mean money," he said sardonically. "I have that now."

"Love," she said impatiently. "You're lonely without it and it makes me sad to see you live each day wondering who's going to hurt you next. My feelings aren't hurt by it because on some level I can empathize, but you're sometimes guarded against me and I adore you as I would my own grandson."

"I no longer think the entire world is a trap. I've grown up," he told her.

"That's good. But forgive me for not quite believing you."

"I'm picking up Gabrielle Royce's call, Cathy."

"Oh." Cathy smiled and gently retreated from the office. "Now I suppose I can start believing you."

Geoffrey sat on the corner of his desk and picked up his phone. "Hey."

"Hey," Gabrielle said back. "Are you busy building megastars?"

"Not at the moment."

"What would you say to driving to Belleza? I'd like to show you something."

He closed his eyes, aware of the calmness waiting to settle in his bones if he'd just let it. If he could just let himself trust what he'd found in her... "Yeah," he said, "I can do that."

"Geoffrey, I—"

"Gabby?"

"Just I'll see you soon."

Maybe, he thought as he left the office and replayed what she'd started to say on the phone, if he let himself trust she would see that it was okay to do the same.

When he arrived at her condo and she opened the door, he felt his disposition change from tense and angry to taken completely aback.

Gabrielle smiled up at him, all shimmer and class in form-fitting dark pants and a baggy sweater that might be made out of gold. She'd pushed up the sleeves and one shoulder was exposed. She'd dragged her gold-dusted auburn hair to one side and had to be elevated five or six inches off the floor in her shoes.

"I'm wearing this to the gala tomorrow night, but I wanted you to be the first one to see me in it." She reached for his necktie and lightly pulled him forward. She smelled like citrus. "Stay the night?"

"I don't want to be anyplace else."

They didn't kiss, but ended up in the bedroom. He looked at the neat bed and did a double take at a bucket of ice sitting on one of her nightstands. "AC problems?"

"Nope. I want to show you something. But I'm going to need your necktie." She waited for him to remove it before she lay it across the bed and then stripped out of the clothes he couldn't wait to see her wearing again tomorrow. "I was thinking that I could give you my trust tonight."

Geoffrey watched her crawl nude onto the bed. He'd recognize her cute ass anywhere. He'd traced her tattoo with his tongue the first time he'd seen it. He was hooked on her laugh. "Trust isn't tangible, Gabby."

"It is. Open yourself to it." She pointed to the bucket. "I'm going to let you blindfold me and touch me with just the ice. I'm going to trust you."

A shiver spread across his back like wings, and he hadn't even touched the ice. But as she leaned forward and waited for him to blindfold her with his tie, he was eager to experiment.

Sex flavored with trust. This would be new for him.

"Have you done this before?" he asked, careful not to touch her, aware of her tightening nipples and the leap of her fingers against the covers.

"No."

He reached into the bucket for a cube of ice and saw her head turn in the direction of the bucket. She couldn't see him, couldn't predict what he'd do with the ice.

Holding it over her, he tightened his fist around it until cool drops of water splashed onto her navel. She flinched and gasped, and then he grinned as he slid the slick cube up her abdomen to her throat and across her lips.

Geoffrey traced her body with a cube in each hand, and then took a fresh one into his mouth, sucked on it, took it out and then kissed her lips.

She sighed, the heat of her mouth colliding with the chill of his. Still blindfolded, she wrapped her arms around him and they kissed until there was nothing but heat between them.

When he withdrew, it was to tease her nipples with ice and to introduce his arctic kiss to the hot dampness between her thighs. She fumbled to hold his head steady but threw up her hands and sighed. "I trust you to take care of me."

And he did. Twice before he let her peel off the blindfold.

"Trust between two people is supposed to be reciprocated," she told him when her breathing steadied again and she had him on his back in the middle of the bed. "So let me blindfold you now."

"Is this no different than sex in the dark?" he asked her as she swept up the tie.

"It's different. Trust me." Winking, she reached forward and took away his sight. "Lie down. I'm going to take your clothes off. All of them."

Hearing her whisper what she was going to do had him tingling with anticipation. The tingle ran from his scalp to his spine every time she got close to whispering in his ears.

"I'm going to undo your belt…and unzip you…"

Oh, damn, this is surreal. Sensations zigzagged across him, pierced him, and he couldn't control his body. His hands flexed on the bed when he felt her weight leave the bed. "Where are you going?"

"Shh. Trust me."

Another woman might snap pictures and hold them for blackmail or revenge. Another might rifle through his wallet. But not her. He trusted her.

He found the aroma of citrus in the air before he felt her return to the bed.

"Trust me," she said now, and he felt her fingertips on his naked chest. A sheet of soft, fragrant curls brushed him. Her beautiful hair. "Geoffrey, I'm going to blow you. But you have to keep the blindfold in place."

"Okay."

But was it? Did he really trust her to suck him to complete pleasure when he couldn't see what she was doing and couldn't guide her head as she took him?

He felt her tongue on his thighs, then something snug and supple and wet circled his penis.

"What is that?"

"What is what?"

"Whatever you just wrapped around my cock."

"Don't take off the blindfold. If I show you what I'm doing, you're going to get distracted. Trust me, remember?" She kissed his tip. "Trust me. Just trust me."

Geoffrey's flesh tingled everywhere now. He was dangled over the edge of panic and each time he prepared to pull off the blindfold and find out what the hell was going on, she tightened that juicy ring around his shaft and sucked him in tandem.

And then, when he started to feel heavy with pressure and his hips started to piston, she said, "Take off the blindfold. Watch."

He dragged off the tie and reared up on his elbows, and there she was working him with…

"A grapefruit?" The words barely jumped from his lips before she snatched off the citrus ring and replaced it with her mouth, and in seconds he groaned and gave her everything.

She found her way into his arms, kissing his chest. "Was that your first grapefruit job?" His expression made her laugh against his skin. "Now do you get why I couldn't let you see it too soon?"

"You said you don't use food for sex play."

"I don't. Well, I didn't before tonight. I had extra fruit on hand. Oh, we're having oranges for breakfast."

She sat up and when he reached for her, she shook her head. "Shower first. There are places on my anatomy that grapefruit shouldn't contact."

"All right. But you're coming with me." Kissing her, he picked her up and brought her to the bathroom.

"I need a *Who's Who* of the Hollywood elite to navigate this party," Robyn confided to Gabrielle as they stood among a group of Belleza employees gathered near a lighted cerulean pool. The outdoor space was expertly adorned in lights and silk. The sun was gently bleeding over the jagged line of mountain. The private party had launched almost an hour ago with violinists and guitarists and drummers on point. Compliments were already rolling in for the appetizers Gabrielle and her team had prepared. Guests were still arriving in anything from limos to sports cars to luxury Hummers.

"Champagne, girls?" Kimberly said, looking stunning in a plum gown, presenting a bottle in one hand and a tray of flutes in the other. "A toast to another success. The Belleza Resort and Spa isn't cursed. It's blessed."

"Agreed," Robyn decided. The pop of rich red in her dress complemented her skin tone and was as beautiful as the sunset. "Cheers!"

"Cheers." Gabrielle accepted a flute of bubbly. She and her friends took a few minutes to catch up and then Jaxon Dunham swept his fiancée away in the fray of dancers. Having accepted that Geoffrey would be too preoccupied with his guests to steal moments with her, she was dumbstruck when he came to her and kissed her in front of his clients and colleagues and competition. Cameras flashed in the night and she didn't care. Even when she noticed the guest of honor dancing with the Pearl's hostess, she didn't hurry over to block their interaction. She was in the outfit she'd worn for Geoffrey last night and all she could think about was finding herself bare flesh to bare flesh in his arms again.

"I didn't think we'd get a chance to dance tonight," she commented as he held her.

"You made this possible. You had a vision and are as controlling as I am. If I can't dance with you, what the hell am I doing?"

"I'm happy, Geoffrey."

"Me, too."

They danced through the next song, until someone tapped their shoulders. "Can I cut in? She's the prettiest woman here."

Gabrielle eased away from Geoffrey and gaped at the tall, almost regal and equally ruthless man separating them. "*Josh?* What are you doing here?"

"My firm represents one of the labels here tonight." He held out his arms for a long moment. "Are you going to leave me hanging like this, Gabby, or are you going to give me that dance you owe me?"

"Who is this?" she heard Geoffrey say as she was twirled into the other man's arms.

"Geoffrey, this is Josh Royce." She refused to dissolve in tears at being confronted in public, at being forced to be civil for the sake of protecting the man she loved. "He's my brother."

"I think you're acquainted with my law firm, Girard. My client and my team are looking forward to seeing you in court."

Gabrielle knew her eyes were round with surprise. "Court?"

"His client is the label that coerced one of my clients to be in breach of contract—"

"What?" she screeched, but Josh was already talking over her, snuffing out her voice, like always.

"Girard, Girard, come on, man. Save the accusations for the court. This is a party, isn't it? Celebrate Phenom Jones's success and find someone to dance with who isn't my sister."

"Your sister's my date tonight."

"I'm familiar with how you work. Don't think you can make my sister one of your discards."

"Stop," she said, her teeth grinding together. "Both of you. I'm literally caught in the middle of this, and I don't want to be."

Josh's dancing ceased, but he still held on to her possessively. "What have you been doing out here, Gabby? Have you been sleeping with this guy?"

"I'm with him, Josh. If you'd cared to show interest in my life, I might feel comfortable updating you and the family more often."

"I'll forgive the backtalk this time. Another thing— I don't think Mom and Dad care for updates on the men you happen to be screwing."

She pushed him away and was fully prepared to deck him if tried to grab her. Just like her family to intrude on something good in her life and exploit it. She rushed over to Robyn.

"That's your brother?" Robyn asked.

"Yes. As destructive as ever. I can't… Of course he'd show up here. Of course something horrible would happen. I was too thrilled with the night."

"Don't talk that way."

Robyn didn't know. They'd been friends since boarding school, but she just didn't know how deeply the Royces could cut.

"What you're doing with my sister? It ends now," Josh said, darting his head as he spoke in that threatening voice all her brothers and her father shared.

The music continued, but conversations around them tapered off and Gabrielle caught the glimmer of camera flashes.

No...

"Gabby told me her family didn't support her dreams. Look at what she's made of herself here. Can't you be proud of that?"

"Proud that my sister's some roughneck record producer's groupie of the night? Not really."

Gabrielle rubbed her temples. "You were saying, Robyn?"

"It doesn't matter. How can the two of you be from the same family?"

Geoffrey grunted a laugh at Josh. "You're a miserable human being, but don't put that misery on Gabby. She deserves better."

"She has the best. People have been handing her success all her life. She's a spoiled princess. She hasn't accomplished anything other than holding on to the gig her rich bestie gave her!"

Geoffrey frowned and she saw doubt in his eyes. "Gabby?"

"Kim Parker and my sister and...where's the other one? Oh, there she is. Robyn Henderson. The three of them have been friends since they went to this all-girls prep school back East. My sister's the top chef here because Kim handed her the job."

Gabrielle was too stunned to defend herself or attempt to separate the lies from truth. "I can't stand around and watch this," she told Robyn. "I'll be in the kitchen." Her friend let her go and she moved as swiftly as her shoes would let her.

She found excuses to stay indoors over the next few hours. For her, the night was ruined, but maybe with her out of the way things had smoothed over and when she finally reemerged she'd find Geoffrey waiting to hold her close and tell her again that he was thankful for her.

Cute fantasy, but how likely is that *to happen?*

"I still don't believe in the curse of the Belleza," she said aloud, and only a line cook nearby grunted in agreement. "I just want to believe in love."

Eventually, Geoffrey came to her. By then she'd gotten word that the party was fizzling and guests were generally pleased and moving on. When he stepped into the kitchen, she rushed him for a kiss.

"I knew you'd come." But his hands hardly held her and the kiss was one-sided. "Geoffrey?"

"Why didn't you tell me you were from a wealthy family or that you went to prep school or that you're friends with the family that owns this place?"

"None of it affects what we have," she reasoned. "I know you asked before and I skirted around it, but I never lied."

"You did. A lie of omission is a lie. If you don't know that, then we have a hell of a problem, don't you think?"

She released him. "Hey, if you're taking your anger

at Josh out on me, all that's going to do is hurt me. He'll be fine. We're not close."

"That'll change when you finish playing chef and go back to the family fold, though, right?" His eyes were impossibly cold for a summer California night. "Your brother's confident that you're going through a phase and will come to your senses when you realize what's important. He seems to think you want someone with the same breeding as yours. He seems to think you're only playing at being a chef, and playing me."

"He's wrong."

"He's not wrong about prep school and your friendship with the Parkers."

"Well, no, but—"

"I fell for this. I fell in love with you, Gabby, and what I loved was a lie. This is friggin' unbelievable." Holding up his hands, he backed away and shoved out of the kitchen.

Spinning around, she found the line cook there with open arms, and she cried on his shoulder.

"Aw, Gabby, it's an argument. He'll miss you in no time. He'll be back."

"No," she said, sniffling. "I'm going after him. My brother."

Gabrielle recruited Kimberly to help her find Josh. He'd rented a room at the resort overnight, so she had no trouble finding him and going straight to his door. "You had no right," she said calmly as she walked into his room. None of her brothers responded to raised voices or threats. "No right to strut into my life and exploit me at a high-profile gala. Mom and Dad wouldn't approve of that."

Josh conceded with, "That's true. I apologize if my temper—"

"It's not your temper. It's your personality. This is who you are. You want to elevate yourself by climbing on others, and I will have no part of it. I live here now and this is my life now. I'm an accomplished chef. I've worked damn hard to get where I am, and simply because someone offered me a chance doesn't mean I haven't struggled to make something solid of that chance. Tell me you understand."

"I could tell you that and lie to you, or I could give you the truth."

"Josh, even if you and the family don't accept my career, you need to respect my relationship with Geoffrey. I love him. He loves me. That's a miracle."

"It's not. It's sex."

"He left me tonight because you told him that I'm only playing him. How could you make that accusation when you don't even know me anymore?" She jammed her fists to her hips. "Oh, but you're the lawyer so proud of manipulating another record label's client. I guess it's my fault for expecting you to have integrity when you wouldn't know ethics if it bit you on the ass."

"Are you done with this childish tirade of yours?"

"Almost." She walked to him. "I love you and the rest of the family, but I will *never* forgive you for your behavior. If Mom and Dad somehow are aware of your coming here and spying on me, tell them that if I'd been thinking about coming back to the fold, I wouldn't now. It won't happen."

"They don't know. I didn't know you were with Geoffrey Girard until I saw you with him. My client's dispute with his label? It's business. Worry about yours and I'll worry about mine." Josh opened the door before she could slam out of the room. "Gabby, when you think about it, really, it didn't take much to make him walk away."

Chapter 11

Gabrielle hadn't turned off her phone, but she wasn't answering his calls. For the first couple of days, Geoffrey had thought it smartest to give her the space she evidently wanted. When three days had passed without his hearing her voice or seeing her walk past him with that perky bop in her step and the adventure hunger in her beautiful brown eyes, he got the feeling that he was losing her.

He'd blown up at her the other night without giving her a chance to talk, and in that way he'd been as much of an asshole as her brother. As he drove to the place where he knew he'd find her—home—his mind replayed clips of their time together. Great sex, even better conversation and above even that was peace.

Geoffrey had known peace when he was with Gabrielle. He couldn't give it up without trying to fight for it first.

He carried a dozen white roses into the Pearl and stopped at the hostess's desk. "Charlene, hi."

"Hi. How many florists did you put in the black buying all those flowers?" She must've noticed the apprehension on his face. "You're looking for Gabby Royce. She's gone. Took a vacation to get away from all the negativity."

"Damn," he muttered, and defeat hit him hard.

"Kidding! She's here." The hostess grinned, but it dropped when he glared at her. "She's preparing a menu, but I can get her. I promise, I only mean to help this time. What can I do?"

Geoffrey thought quickly, and when Charlene went to retrieve Gabby, he set the roses on a table and went back to the entrance and waited. He saw the pair of women emerge from the kitchen and navigate the dining room. The memory of the first day he'd eaten here came rushing back.

Once again she didn't see him. She was so focused on her job. So committed to the career she loved.

He loved her. No matter what she decided about her future with him, he had to tell her that he loved her and he was sorry. But talking wouldn't get her attention. He'd tried to talk, but she wouldn't pick up his call.

This time he wouldn't talk.

As he saw her slowly approach the table piled high with roses, and the hostess turned back to give him a thumbs-up, he stepped forward and began to sing. It was the R&B single he'd recorded and released before he'd shifted to producing. At his private studio, he'd been irked to hear the song but she'd drawn him into a dance and quietly demanded that he not deprive her of the chance to know that part of his past.

Gabrielle turned and bumped the table, and some roses bounced onto the floor. Her mouth shaped the words, "Oh, my God."

Guests scooted around in their chairs and some held up their phones to capture the moment, and he knew that this would be the wisest decision he'd made in a long time, or the biggest failure.

But she was worth every wait and worth every risk.

There was no back track to help him, nothing to enhance the effect. He was a man asking his woman to stop and listen. As he continued to sing, he held out a hand for hers.

She didn't lay her hand in his. She threw her arms over his shoulders, and he banded an arm around her waist and they rocked together to the ballad until he stopped singing and dared to kiss her.

Applause circled them. Parting, he let her swipe a rose from the pile and then he led her through the dining room and out of the restaurant.

Outside, he hugged her and apologized. "I was so wrong. If I could kick my own ass, I'd do it."

She laughed. Oh, God, that laugh. He didn't deserve it, but he selfishly let it restore the peace in his soul. "Kicking yourself won't be necessary. I do believe you're sorry and I accept the apology."

"I love you, Gabby. It hurt, though, that you didn't trust me with the truth."

"Would you have come to love me if you'd known the truth from the beginning? I doubt it."

Geoffrey nodded. As shameful as it was, it was the truth. "I was too hung up on the fantasy of you as someone like me—self-made. From that first day, I knew you were different and I thought the difference was that you didn't have this life handed to you. Who am I to judge you for how you found this career?"

"It's not that I didn't trust you. Eventually, I really did. But it seemed too late to try to go back and say, 'Oh, by the way, I come from a wealthy and prominent family that's all but disowned me and one of my best friends hired me at this resort.' I'd hoped that you loved me for me, not because of where you thought I came from."

His reaction to the truth about her revealed some truths about him. "I was so damn wrong and I don't think I deserve you now, but stay, Gabby. Stay in love with me."

"I am." She tightened her hold. "I love you and I'm not walking away. But you have to know that I'm not the person you first thought I was or the person my brother made me out to be. I need to show you, so come with me." Her gaze touched his thoughtfully. "Trust me?"

Taking him home might be the silliest mistake of the summer, but Gabrielle could think of no other way to illustrate to him the truth. She was a Royce by blood, but not in spirit. She marched to the beat of her heart, not to the dictatorship of her father. She didn't follow in her brothers' footsteps or fall in line behind her mother.

To reveal the truth to Geoffrey, she'd brought him to her parents' home. Once she'd belonged here, but that was before she'd become whom she wanted to be.

The palatial estate with its dozens of staff and unapproachable vibe was as Gabrielle had remembered. She tucked her hand in Geoffrey's as they approached the threatening main building. She didn't need a man to hold her hand, but it felt good to touch him.

"Big house, small-minded people," she said, neither angry nor sad. She had long ago accepted her family for what they were: unaccepting of her. "Are you ready for this?"

In answer, he rapped on the door with the antique knocker.

A butler answered but didn't let them inside. Instead, he shut the door and a moment later her mother opened the door again.

"Gabrielle."

"Mom."

"Who's this?" Gabrielle's mother appraised Geoffrey quickly. "An answer, someone?"

"Mom, this is Geoffrey Girard. According to Josh, who behaved terribly at a party in Belleza where I live and work, Geoffrey's the man I'm currently sleeping with. According to me, he's the man I love." She laid her hand over his chest. "Geoffrey, this is my mother—"

"Mrs. Royce. Let's not forget our manners, shall we, Gabrielle? I'll get Mr. Royce. Step inside, I suppose." When the stately woman rushed through the foyer, she pivoted so fast that her high heels screeched on the polished floor. "Oh, stay there, would you? The floors were just done."

"In case you didn't pick up on it," Gabrielle told him, "that was Mom's way of *not* inviting us in. When I was growing up, she would say that to people she didn't want inside the house. It was her signature brushoff move."

"And she'd use it on her own kid?"

"The consequences of disobeying her and Dad."

Mrs. Royce returned to the elegant foyer accompanied by her husband, a reed-thin, mustached man.

"I'll be damned," Mr. Royce said, turning to his wife. "She looks unrefined."

"She's been living like a vagrant since she left the Academy, dear."

Gabrielle jerked her hands in the air. "*She* is standing two feet away from you. I have not been living like a vagrant. I was in cooking school and researching and working my way up in the culinary world. You both are fully damn aware of it."

Her mother winced at the word *damn*.

"Watch your mouth," her father warned. "We open our home to you and you come to us speaking like that? If you want your place in this family back, understand that I won't tolerate that."

"Dad, I don't want 'my place' back. All you and Mom want to do is put me in what you think is my place. I don't fit. I don't fit in a family that spits on self-expression and tries to dash the hopes of someone who wants more out of life than to follow your orders. I have a real life in Belleza. I have someone now." She pointed to Geoffrey. "This is Geoffrey Girard. He's a music producer."

"An entertainer?" Mrs. Royce wrinkled her nose. "Oh, Gabrielle."

"I own a company I built from the ground up, Mrs. Royce," he said. "I can afford to buy your house and turn it into a strip mall. But I don't use money for vendettas. I *can,* however, take care of your daughter. And I intend to."

"Take care of her? By letting her serve people food

for a living? That's not the life we want for her. My lord, just look at her hands!"

Gabrielle raised a brow at her simple, clean hands. Sure, there were scars from kitchen accidents over the years, but she didn't regard a hand neglected of an expensive manicure to be an offensive one. "Nail polish and false nails are no good in my line of work, Mom."

"That'd change if you'd stop being silly and move back home," her father said.

"Earning my own living isn't being silly, Dad."

And soon she was like a tennis ball sailing over a net. First her mother would launch a verbal attack. Then her father. Back and forth. It came to the point that she'd prefer to hunker down and cover her ears, but maturity demanded that she face them coolly and clarify her position. "I have no intention of moving back into this house. I brought Geoffrey here to show him how little I have in common with my family."

In minutes they were outside again, and she was shut out of her family's world again. It was unfortunate but didn't hurt as much as she'd feared it might.

"That was brave as hell, facing them like that," Geoffrey told her as they began to put the Royce family estate behind them.

"That back there? That's where I come from. It's not who I am, Geoffrey."

"I know." He edged closer and slowly, easily kissed her under the sunshine and blue skies. "I love you for you. I want to be your family. I want to marry you, Gabrielle."

Marry. You.

"Marry me?" she cried. "Oh, God. Then I'd officially be off the shelf."

"The day we met at the Pearl, that was your last day on the shelf." Winking, he slipped something from his pocket and lowered to one knee. "I want to do this right. I want to marry you, Gabrielle Royce. I don't care if it's a huge wedding or if we elope. And I wouldn't care if you wore Chuck Taylor high-tops under your dress."

She laughed. Then tears welled and she didn't know whether to blot her eyes or lean down and kiss him stupid.

"Swear you'll laugh every day we're together."

"That might be a long time."

"I'm hoping it'll be forever."

She gestured to her parents' silent estate. "I come with those people. They probably won't ever welcome you to the family. How do you feel about that?"

"I'm marrying *you*. If you say yes." He opened a deep blue crushed velvet box and the sunshine beamed down on a breathtaking diamond that lacked a band. "I was thinking you'd want to customize the band, so to give you a blank slate, I bought the diamond."

She sobbed and laughed. "When did you do this?"

"When you weren't answering my calls. I'd hoped you would forgive me." He took her hand, kissed each finger and lightly bit the ring finger. "So, do you want to do this? For better or for worse, with me?"

"Yes," she whispered, bending to kiss him. "For better or for worse."

Gabrielle stepped into the Ruby Retreat to find Robyn, Kimberly and Jaxon already there. They'd agreed to meet for drinks and wedding planning. "Sorry I'm late!"

"You've been late all week," Kimberly commented good-naturedly. She turned to smooch her man on the lips. "I know what it's like to have someone keeping you awfully busy."

"I'm not going to comment on that," Jaxon said, but he returned her kiss with zest that the entire room could likely feel.

"Shame on y'all," Robyn said with a smile.

"Geoffrey and I have been sort of celebrating something all week," Gabrielle said gently. "We're engaged."

"What?" Robyn and Kimberly shrieked. "You're getting married?"

"Yes! He bought a stunning diamond but I'm Gabby-fying the band. His suggestion." She held out her arms wide for a hug. Kim and Robyn flocked to her, squealing congrats. "You get over here, too, Jaxon. I want all the love!"

Within minutes they had drinks on the house and the congratulations were beginning to filter in. Someone had alerted the Pearl and in shifts the staff were coming up to hug her and remind her of her embarrassing misadventures in casual dating. She slipped away from the craziness to text message her fiancé. She'd left his bed to shower and drive here. She was only a little bit guilty that in the back of her mind she was counting the hours until she'd be back in that man's bed…back in his arms.

Your place tonight?

Geoffrey responded straightaway. I have natural spring water ice and a big bucket.

Gabrielle smirked naughtily as she tapped her reply,

already imagining what she'd do when she got her hands on the ice and on him. I'll bring a grapefruit.

As she was putting her smartphone in her bag, she noticed Robyn several feet away leaning over her own phone before pressing it to her ear and whispering. Gabrielle wanted to move, but her sneakers wouldn't go. She was still standing there when Robyn turned, saw her and lowered the device.

"Everything okay?" Gabrielle asked, feeling a prickly chill she didn't like.

"Oh, that? Yeah. Yes." Robyn scoffed. "Wrong number. C'mon, let's get back. Now there are *two* weddings to plan."

Gabrielle let her friend precede her, and she glanced around the room, not quite sure what she was looking for. So strange, things were new, and yet still familiar. She still loved this place and these people.

"I still don't believe in the curse of the Belleza," she said under her breath as she returned to her friends and their celebratory drinks. "But I believe in love."

* * * * *

This summer is going to be hot, hot, hot
with a new miniseries
from fan-favorite authors!

YAHRAH ST. JOHN
LISA MARIE PERRY
PAMELA YAYE

**HEAT WAVE
OF DESIRE**

Available June 2015

**HOT SUMMER
NIGHTS**

Available July 2015

**HEAT OF
PASSION**

Available August 2015

California Desert Dreams

HARLEQUIN®
www.Harlequin.com

KPHSNC0615

REQUEST YOUR FREE BOOKS!

2 FREE NOVELS
PLUS 2 FREE GIFTS!

KIMANI™ ROMANCE

Love's ultimate destination!

KROM15